THE ELEAGON SAGA: BOOK ONE

A.R. HOFF

Copyright 2021

This is a work of fiction. Names, characters, places, and incidents are a product of the author's imagination or used fictitiously and are not to be construed as real. Any resemblance to actual events, places, organizations, or persons living or dead is entirely coincidental.

To my chaos of a family, I dedicate this book. To my eleagons Chadrick, Maverick and Brodrick, who even stopped eating brownies to read my book, every day is an adventure that I am proud to be on. To the love of my life, my strength, my anchor, my grounding point, my husband Chad. To my amazing mom and dad who have given more than any daughter could ask for. To my sisters, Tara, Kimberly, and Maegan, my childhood was brighter with you.

TABLE OF CONTENTS

PROLOGUE 1
CHAPTER 1 - THE PENDANT 5
CHAPTER 2 - BREA 199
CHAPTER 3 - BLAZE 377
CHAPTER 4 - THE WOODS 44
CHAPTER 5 - ELDRAGOR 61
CHAPTER 6 - THE BASICS 68
CHAPTER 7 - AEROIOUS 75
CHAPTER 8 - STUDENTS 84
CHAPTER 9 - THE WORTHINESS CEREMONY 96
CHAPTER 10 - SETTLING IN 104
CHAPTER 11 - DAY ONE 117
CHAPTER 12 - HOROLOGY 137
CHAPTER 13 - MORE OBBLES 149
CHAPTER 14 - TERERBIS 157
CHAPTER 15 – BREWTION 164
CHAPTER 16 - PROPHECIES 173
CHAPTER 17- NIGHTMARES 185
CHAPTER 18 - VULKAN 188

CHAPTER 19 - SKELETON KEY 195

CHAPTER 20 - VEIL OF DARKNESS 199

CHAPTER 21 - VOROUS BEAST 207

CHAPTER 22 - CONGRATULATIONS 214

CHAPTER 23 - SPIXIE CARAVAN 218

CHAPTER 24 - WHICH PATH TO TAKE 232

CHAPTER 25 - ALL WILL BE REVEALED 237

CHAPTER 26 - IS IT TRUE? 247

PROLOGUE

You must save the child!

The words hammered through Tabi's mind as she fluttered over the crying newborn baby, who was swaddled in a tattered purple banner. Taking a deep breath, the dainty teapot-sized creature closed her violet eyes and clasped her hands together. As this guardian spixie of Eldragor whispered the secret enchantment, her hands began to glow. Keeping her fingers laced, she moved her hands in a circular motion above her long purple hair, creating a shower of shimmering purple mist. As Tabi twirled in the mist, she grew to the size of a small human, landed on uneasy legs, withdrew her wings, and gazed at the precious child. "We must hurry if you are to survive," she whispered.

Tabi took one final look around the room before grabbing the baby by its tattered swaddle and running out of the study and into the outer chamber. The wind howled through the broken section of the massive stained-glass dome overhead. The castle's thick stone walls groaned around her. Her tiny heart pounded rapidly in her chest as she shielded the baby with her small body and darted into the hallway and down the stairs while dodging broken chunks of stone and glass that fell around her like rain, cutting her skin in several places. The pain was nothing compared to the anguish of her broken heart.

In the hallway below, she passed other people running in a panic. Tabi finally reached a door and ran out, but halted abruptly as she gazed at the massive roots that slithered around the ancient stone statues before pulverizing them to rubble.

Screams erupted in the distance, and above a dark cloud spit out huge hailstones.

"The Rift," Tabi whispered, snuggling the bundle closer to her body. "It's begun."

A thick piece of acidic hail fell on a nearby stone, pulling Tabi out of her thoughts as it sizzled and melted in front of her. The high pitch screams echoed in her ears.

Soon she approached the forest's edge. The trees were gnarled and turning black. She had no time to be afraid and plunged right into the dense wood. After a few minutes of running in the forest, a large root suddenly ripped from the ground in front of her.

Tabi thrust one hand toward the plant, unleashing a flurry of purple dust that burned the vine into a blackened husk. She turned her head, spotting another one slithering toward her. As she began to summon dust again, Tabi saw a shadowy creature behind her and ran in terror.

Out of breath and near exhaustion after her long sprint, Tabi burst into a clearing. Her heart sank at the sight; the spixie village was nearly destroyed. As fear and dread overcame her, she saw that the caravan she most needed was still mostly standing. Tabi ran inside a brass-painted one that had a huge compass on the top and the words Hendy's Lost and Found on the side.

Tabi flicked her glowing wrist and slammed the door shut against the force of the wind. A wooden bar fell into place, locking them in. The door and then the whole caravan groaned against an outside force that was not the wind.

Brushing aside maps and tools from the surface of the table, Tabi quickly set the swaddled baby down and took a deep breath. Looking around, she found what she needed: Hendry's old compass, which was still in its spot of honor in the glass display case. Lifting the top of the enclosure with one hand, Tabi retrieved the worn compass while the caravan shook from the assault of the shadowy creature.

Tabi pulled a seed from her pocket, placed it inside the compass, and grabbed the swaddled child. The needle spun into action, spinning around and around. A root grew from the bottom of the instrument and attached itself to the wooden planks of the floor. She gazed wide-eyed and took a hesitant step backward as branches grew out the top of the compass, reached out toward her, coiled around her wrist, and suddenly retracted. The spixie squeezed her bundle tight as the branch pulled her into the compass. Twisting and turning, she floated through darkness, still gripping the branch. After what seemed like forever, a tear in the darkness appeared.

Tabi flopped out onto the wet grassy ground. Her eyes adjusted to a large oak tree as lightning lit the area and thunder roared. She stood, holding the bundle in her arms fiercely.

The infant cried. Tabi squinted, trying to see through, and was rewarded with the sight of a large house nearby. Nearing the porch, she flicked her wrist, sending purple sparks to the doorbell, which caused its chime to ring out against the growing ferocity of the storm. The baby wailed as the wind picked up.

Tabi leaned over the infant one last time, fingers trembling and leaving flakes of purple spixie dust behind. With a heavy sigh, she left the child under a large flowerless rose bush near the porch as its cries echoed in the wind.

"You must stay away," she whispered.

A warm yellow light illuminated the white wooden porch and the door opened to reveal a woman wearing a yellow raincoat and boots. As the woman walked down the front steps toward the sound of the cries, Tabi whispered, "Remember you are the child that withstood the tempest; the child that saved us!

CHAPTER 1 - THE PENDANT

"**S**NAKE! SNAKE!" The frantic shriek disrupted the peaceful summer afternoon of twelve-year-old Daxton Tanner. This wasn't the first time he heard the familiar scream about a snake, and he doubted it would be the last. Opening his eyes, he sat up to watch a flighty red-haired, short, pudgy woman bolt past him while tripping over her own two feet before reaching the back screen door.

The mid-afternoon wind picked up as Daxton made his way to the old Tudor-style house. He could hear the frantic voices through the open windows. Slowly he crossed the lawn, his blue eyes roamed across an old sign that read, Sister Orphanage.

They sure don't act like sisters, Daxton thought.

Daxton was the oldest of the five orphans that currently lived at the Sister Orphanage. He knew he didn't look like it; he was small and skinny and the hand-me-down clothing never fit him right. He looked like a poor, homely child and his unkempt blonde hair didn't help with his appearance either.

"PAT JENKINS! There's no SNAKE!" was all Daxton heard when he opened the screen door.

This is going to be interesting.

"I swear, you'll be the death of me one day!" Thelma said, wiping a glob of batter from her cheek. Thelma Jenkins was a very practical southern woman, unlike her sister. She was tall, with a long face and green eyes. Her brown hair was always in a bun to beat the summer heat of the south.

"There's never a snake! You start shouting, we all go look, and there is no snake!" Thelma fussed. "Just look at this mess!"

If anyone can make a mess and irritate Thelma at the same time, it's Pat.

Daxton looked at the cake batter on the floor before his eyes fell upon a ghostly-looking Pat. She was having another one of her episodes. For as long as he could remember, Pat would see things that were not there.

Pat Jenkins, who was shorter than her sister, was the least practical person he knew. She also had green eyes and a pudgy face with freckles that danced across her ivory nose. On a good day, she'd be in her garden planting.

Today is not a good day.

"Where did you see it?" Daxton asked, curiosity getting the better of him.

"Behind the big oak," Pat replied, "It was long and black and…."

"Oh, for heaven's sake, Daxton Tanner!" Thelma said, picking up the cake pan off the floor. "You should know better than to feed Pat's imagination. It only makes her worse."

Worse than what; a woman losing her mind?

Daxton lowered his eyes. He wanted to walk out the back door, but with the mess in the kitchen he knew that wasn't going to happen.

"Don't just stand there, get the mop." Thelma scowled.

More chores!

"Yes, ma'am," Daxton said, his eyes cast low.

Thelma was right, however. He had been told many times not to give in to Pat when she 'saw' things, but he couldn't help it. Curiosity got the better of him every time. It was probably why the interviews with possible parents never went right. He always asked the wrong questions.

Pat took a seat in one of the mismatched chairs around the old oak table and folded her arms and crossed her legs. "Thelma," Pat started in a soft voice, straightening her shoulders.

She's not going to let this go.

"ENOUGH! There is NO SNAKE!" Thelma yelled.

Daxton jumped at the sound of Thelma's voice. When she yelled like this, it meant she was at her wit's end. It didn't happen often, but when it did, Daxton had the urge to turn invisible. He didn't know whether to hide under the table or continue mopping.

Hiding would probably make her madder, he thought as he stood there, waiting for more bickering to come, but there was a moment of silence. *That wasn't good. Silence in this place always meant something was going to happen, and it usually wasn't good.*

Continuing to mop, his left palm began to feel a light burn, like he was holding his palm over a candle.

What is wrong with my hand? Maybe it's a bug bite.

The pain grew so much he dropped the mop; it was as if the wood burned him.

"You okay?" Thelma asked, looking at him with concern.

"Yeah, slipped," Daxton answered, picking up the mop off the ground.

Daxton looked at his hand and saw a small welt in the shape of a triangle. His eyes grew wide, but he didn't want to bring more attention to himself; not while Thelma was on the warpath.

This is weird. Add this to the list of why people don't want me.

"Look, Pat, you're obviously seeing things again," Thelma noted in a gentle tone. "I'll make another appointment to check your medications."

Great, she had to mention medications!

Pat shot her sister an indignant glare. "My medications are just fine, Thelma! Just because no one else has seen the snake doesn't mean it's not real," Pat countered.

"Goodness, Pat, really? That's exactly the reason it's not real!" Thelma looked at her sister, not unkindly. "You could make sure the kids are packed for camp instead of wasting your time screaming about some stupid snake that doesn't exist!"

And there it is!

"No one! And I mean NO ONE tells me what to do!" Pat cried, standing and waltzing out the back screen door.

That didn't go well. But when does it?

Daxton mopped up almost the last of the cake batter on the floor when a roar of activity erupted behind him.

"Where's the snake?" Isaac asked, excitement shining in his hazel eyes as he raised his pet frog. "Fred needs a brother. I could, uh, maybe I could keep the snake as a pet?"

Isaac Matthews was nine and had red hair and as many freckles across his nose as the frog had spots on its skin. He loved animals and wanted to make them all his family. It made every day a little more fun and interesting when Isaac found a new creature.

"It might eat him," Daxton stated, raising an eyebrow.

"He would not. They would be family," Isaac said.

"Isaac, how many times have I told you about that frog?" Thelma scolded.

"Well, he's my brother and I need to keep him safe," Isaac replied, looking a little upset.

That's Isaac for you.

"Furthermore, there is no snake!" Thelma repeated, looking at him crossly. "Also, the frog is not your brother! Now, put that frog back outside and help Daxton clean up the rest of this mess. You are getting dirt everywhere."

Just as Isaac was about to hide the frog inside his overalls pocket, it sprang from his little hand right into the cake pan and then leaped on the countertop, leaving globs of batter where it landed.

Can today get any worse?

Thelma hollered, dropping the cake pan. Isaac dove to the countertop trying to catch the frog, while Daxton watched as the littlest orphan came running in with a rusty bucket. Elizabeth Clearwater, age four, was no taller than three feet. The small girl had raven black hair, blue eyes, and rosy skin. Sometimes it looked like she could see through you.

Elizabeth went sliding and landed on her bottom. Her bucket went flying as the cake batter frog jumped into her lap. "Get it off me!" Elizabeth yelled.

"Catch that frog!" yelled Thelma, wiping cake batter off her for the second time that hour.

Daxton grabbed Elizabeth's bucket and tried to put it over the frog but was too slow. Fred was leaping around the kitchen making a bigger mess as he dragged cake batter with him.

"Daxton, you missed it!" Elizabeth cried.

"Get that thing out of my kitchen!" Thelma ordered, reaching for a broom.

"Don't hurt Fred!" Isaac yelled.

Daxton dove again, but the frog continued to evade him.

With the kitchen in a full-blown panic, the frog disappeared.

As Daxton squatted down looking for Fred, he heard the back screen door slam. He glanced up to see Tiffany in the archway.

Here she comes to save the day.

Tiffany Taylor, second oldest orphan at age twelve, was cradling a precarious load of eggs in her pink basket. Her sapphire eyes locked with Daxton for just a moment before Fred jumped from the countertop onto the top of her big pink bow.

"What! What is that!? Get it off me! GET. IT. OFF. ME!" Tiffany screamed while swinging her pink basket back and forth. With each swing, small brown and white eggs flew out of the basket, landing with a smack on the floor. Daxton's eyes grew wide watching one egg hit the floor, then another. He lunged forward, pulling the bottom of his blue shirt out to catch the newest eggs that escaped Tiffany's basket. To his surprise, they landed one by one with ease in his shirt basket without breaking.

What in the mad science is happening?

Suddenly, two brown eggs left the basket at the same time. He would have to catch one in his hand while getting the other to fall into his shirt. If he was lucky, he could save them both at the same time.

There's a first time for everything.

Daxton reached his left palm out to try to catch one but missed. He was sure it was going to hit the floor. Instead, the small brown egg hovered at the tips of his fingers in the air. His heart raced, the egg still hovering.

I am going crazy. These women have driven me mad.

Tiffany was too busy trying to get the cake batter covered frog off her, and the commotion distracted the other children. Daxton was the only one seeing this. Before he realized what was happening, the egg moved into his hand.

What just happened? Tiffany didn't throw that. None of them did. And why didn't it hit the floor?

Daxton's mind went into overdrive as he moved over to the countertop to heave all the eggs on top, before turning around to watch the commotion.

Tiffany was turning round and round trying to get the frog off the back of her pink shirt. Her tall, lanky frame spinning out of control was another disaster waiting to happen. Without a second thought, Daxton sprung into action again. Grabbing Fred by his back and peeling his tiny green legs from Tiffany's long, blonde hair, Daxton held Fred as the chaos of the kitchen slowly ended.

"You saved Fred!" Isaac said, grabbing the frog and holding him up to his ear for a moment before shoving him into his denim overalls. "He says thank you!"

"You're welcome," Daxton replied.

"That frog does not talk!" Tiffany said, fixing the bow she sewed herself.

"Fred does," Isaac replied, showing his missing tooth with a grin.

Daxton moved over to the sink and heard a squeaky voice behind him. It was Brent Thompson, who was younger than Daxton by a few months, but was the smartest of the three older orphans. He was stocky and short with pale skin and a few faint freckles. The one thing that stood out about him was his big, hazel eyes that were magnified behind a pair of round silver glasses. Brent had a talent for saying the worst possible thing at the worst possible time. Smart? Yes. Wise? Not so much.

"Is the cake done?" Brent asked.

"No, no, and more no," Thelma grumbled, slamming the broom back into its corner. "Isaac, you get that frog out of this kitchen this moment! Elizabeth, go change! Brent, Daxton, and Tiffany, I want this mess cleaned up!"

"Yes, ma'am," the trio begrudgingly replied in unison as Thelma left the kitchen.

"What did you do?" Tiffany asked, glaring at Daxton.

"I didn't do anything," Daxton said.

"I bet we won't get any cake," Tiffany grumbled.

"Thelma sure is upset," Brent replied, pushing his glasses up.

"What gave that away?" Daxton asked, looking at the mess in the kitchen.

If I could go one day without hearing about a snake, it would be a good day.

As evening approached Daxton still had lots of things to do. Tomorrow morning, he would be leaving for summer camp. He quickly rounded the banister and headed upstairs to pack. The paint was peeling on the wall above the stairs, but Daxton thought of it as adding character. Approaching his bedroom, Daxton noticed the door was open even though he knew he had shut it earlier.

Weird things had been happening to him lately and the door opening was nothing new. For a moment he questioned his own mind before he entered his room slowly, expecting things to just start flying toward him. He exhaled as nothing came flying at him, but before he could close his door, it closed behind him, making Daxton jump. This house is really falling apart or I'm losing my mind.

"Odd," he said aloud. His palm started itching like mad, but he didn't think about it as his mind went back to that egg.

I know what I saw. That egg was floating before it moved into my hand. Tiffany was spinning so fast, I guess I could have been disoriented.

Pausing from his thoughts, he glanced out the small window. Pat was outside picking up sticks from around the old maple tree.

Maybe she's looking for the snake again.

Daxton's bedroom, the smallest of the five, was cramped with a twin-size bed that had a patch quilt for a cover, but at least Daxton did not have to share with anyone like the other kids did. Tiffany bunked with Elizabeth, Brent with Isaac. The walls were bare except for the back where his desk sat under a wooden window that he never opened. There was a bookshelf with only a few books and a dresser. On the desk was a wooden sailboat that Brent and Isaac gave him, ready for adventure.

He went to his dresser then pulled out clean clothes to pack for summer camp. Next, he went to the closet and stood on his tiptoes to retrieve his old backpack from the top shelf. The backpack was ratty and ripping at the seams, but he didn't have anything else to put his clothes in. Looking inside, Daxton spotted a hole in the bottom.

Sighing, he sat down at his desk and tried to figure out how to fix the backpack.

Maybe I can get Tiffany to help me sew it back together.

Looking closer at the hole, he realized sewing thread would not be enough.

Suddenly, Daxton's left hand itched again, this time so bad that he put the backpack down and scratched.

Maybe I have a splinter from that mop. It could be the soap, he thought with a frown.

Looking at the weird set of lines on his palm, Daxton reflected on the time Pat told him were palmar flexion creases, the lines that palm-readers used to tell fortunes. His creases were not normal. According to Pat, most people just had a few main lines or a 'W' like shape, but Daxton had a series of rings, lines, and a triangle in the center, which was now a deep red. The lines would connect to the triangle depending on how he moved his fingers and thumb.

Daxton squinted, studying them. He wanted to tell Thelma about them being so dark and itchy but knew that she would just tell him to use some coconut oil.

I'll mess with my hand after I fix the backpack.

After a few minutes of thinking, Daxton proclaimed, "Duct tape! Duct tape can fix my backpack. It fixes everything and Ms. Pat was using it yesterday."

Daxton hurried downstairs to the junk closet where Ms. Pat threw stuff when she was finished with it. Cautiously, he opened the door, afraid the contents would tumble out. Surprisingly, nothing did. Looking in, Daxton was amazed; the closet had been neatly organized. This is what Ms. Thelma meant when she said she was going to clean where no one had cleaned before. It was all organized, except for a roll of duct tape on the floor in the back of the closet where Pat obviously tossed it yesterday. Daxton retrieved the tape but got distracted by a satchel stacked neatly on top of numerous storage containers. Picking it up, he was surprised by its softness. *This looks like it belongs to an adventurer or something.*

"This satchel will be perfect for camp," Daxton whispered to himself. "Surely Ms. Pat won't mind if I borrow it; she always tells us to take whatever is in here when we need it." Not wanting to risk being caught downstairs by Ms. Thelma when he was supposed to be packing, Daxton quickly took the satchel to his room where he sat on his bed and examined it closely.

A sense of excitement coursed through him as he studied the details, namely the triangular buckles that bedecked the satchel.

The secrets it must have held; the books it must have kept!

The bag was heavy, as if something was inside it. His hands quickly unsnapped the first buckle and then the second before pulling back the flap. Daxton's blue eyes anxiously searched the opening, seeking to find out what was inside.

Daxton could see nothing and rubbed his head in confusion before picking up the satchel again. *There must be something inside it.* Daxton turned it around. The back looked just like the front with the same two golden buckles, and his excitement resurfaced as he unlocked the second set. Instead of pulling the flap upward, this flap folded down, and there, behind the flap, was a large book in a hidden pocket.

Daxton tugged the heavy book out onto his desk. It was bound in leather and covered with all sorts of embellishments in gold and different colors of ink, and it looked expensive. There were symbols and triangles on the cover, and even a big eye in the middle, but no words.

He searched the inner pocket, finding an unexpected object tucked into it: a pendant consisting of two golden pyramids connected at their bases. Both pointed ends had golden clasps attached to a chain. The pyramids were not solid but were made up of golden strands that formed smaller pyramids. He could see the hollow inside of the pyramid and was able to peer through to the other side.

Daxton pulled the pendant out and held it up to the light from his window. The dual pyramids glimmered faintly. A thin layer of dust coated the metal, so he blew on it lightly to clean it off, and the pendant flared with lavender light.

Blinking, Daxton shifted the golden chain, so the pyramids nestled in the palm of his other hand. Immediately, his skin tingled, and the pendant beamed so bright that his hand seemed to glow purple with it. Startled, he dropped the pendant on the desk, but his hand still gleamed with color even as he rubbed his palm on his jeans to scrub the glow away. The light faded and he breathed a sigh of relief while searching for a reasonable explanation.

Maybe the lamp light hitting the pendant made the light beam like a prism does. Yeah, that was it.

Satisfied, Daxton looked back at the pendant on his desk. Puffs of white smoke escaped the seams. Uh, what now? More curious than shocked, he watched the smoke fade to reveal a single purple egg suspended atop a cluster of clouds between the two now-open triangles. The clouds floated upward, carrying the purple egg, which was only the size of a hummingbird egg.

Maybe I came from a family of magicians. Is that even what they're called? Mages? Wizards?

His whole body braced for what might happen next; but nothing did. He shook his head. There was no such thing as magic. A loud crack echoed through the room. Daxton jumped up in fright, knocking his chair over. "It's alive," he muttered in a daze. "What's going on? Am I imagining things?"

That seemed like a good explanation at first, but then the egg began to hover right in front of him; too real to be his imagination.

I couldn't make this up.

Daxton gazed at it for a long time with his mouth agape, trying to understand what was happening with the small purple egg. He couldn't believe this was real. No matter how much he tried to blink the egg away, it remained in front of him.

I've always felt different from the other kids at the orphanage, like I don't belong here. Now I have this crazy pendant and a floating egg, but even though it's the weirdest thing that's ever happened to me, it doesn't feel weird. What if I'm from a place where things like this are normal, and my parents are waiting for me there? This could be how I find my way back to them. Or maybe I'm losing my mind, like Ms. Pat.

Daxton's thoughts trailed off. For the first time, he finally found the words to define how he'd felt his whole life: *A child of two worlds.*

CHAPTER 2 – BREA

*C**rack!*

The sound jolted Daxton out of his thoughts and his eyes locked onto the floating egg once more.

Crack!

The egg began to wobble in the clouds. Daxton needed to make sure it was real. He had to know. Slowly, he reached his hand out, twirling his forefinger in the cloud until his fingertips touched the egg.

Crack!

The sound startled him, and he snatched his hand away. He watched with eager eyes as tiny cracks appeared over the egg.

Suddenly, dozens of tiny pieces of eggshell flew at him like an explosion with some smacking Daxton in the face.

"Ouch!" he cried, ducking under his desk.

At this point, nothing surprised him anymore. He wanted to laugh; he wanted to cry; he wanted to run away.

Taking two cautious steps back, Daxton pulled a book from the shelf and held it in front of his body like a shield. After a moment, he nervously knelt to inspect the egg. So far, no scaly green legs had come out to attack him, but he kept his book handy just in case the creature was dangerous.

Two small, white feet pushed through the shell and a long, white tail emerged from the other side. More pieces of the shell broke away, and a silvery-white creature poked its head out and gazed with big aqua eyes at the boy. A tiny bit of the eggshell was stuck to its forehead. In a daze, Daxton tried to pull the piece away and the creature nipped his finger.

"Ouch!" Daxton grunted, jerking his hand back. He stuck his finger in his mouth and sucked on the sore spot, feeling slight relief.

The odd little creature looked like a furry little cloud with four legs and a tail as it tossed its head, flinging the last piece of eggshell onto the floor. It flapped its wings and soared around his room. It was elegant and beautiful as it glided through the air. Daxton couldn't believe how lucky he was to see something like this. If he wasn't seeing it himself, he never would have believed it was possible. It didn't seem real. Soon, the creature landed gently on his bookshelf.

"Wow, you can fly!" Daxton exclaimed, keeping his wide eyes on the creature as it peered around the room from its lofty perch.

"You're not a bird," he added, cocking his head in thought. "So, uh, what are you?"

Not quite a lizard, definitely not a kitten either. Something in the middle.

It shook off a cloud forming on its back before fluffing up its tiny white wings that had the appearance of puffy vapor. Its long snout ended in a triangular nose, and it had several nebulous shapes on the top of its mane. The beast was no bigger than two little cotton balls, and its long, wispy tail writhed back and forth behind it. The creature looked down at Daxton, seemingly ready to attack, but Daxton could tell it was just as afraid of him as he was of it.

"What are you?" Daxton repeated, still unsure if the creature was truly real. "Maybe I'm dreaming?" Daxton slowly extended his hand to the top of the bookcase where the little creature paced.

It moved to Daxton's fingers and sniffed them before placing its paws gently on one. Daxton twitched at the touch and the lightweight creature scurried down his arm. The tiny puffs of breath felt cool on Daxton's warm skin as the creature continued to his shoulder, where it perched. The soft white tail wound around Daxton's neck like a vine. It felt more solid than Daxton expected based on its vaporous form. It felt like dew droplets and slightly dampened the collar of his shirt.

"What are you?" Daxton asked again as wonder swelled in his heart. For the second time, he felt like he stumbled upon something astonishing, yet half-familiar, as though part of him had always expected this. He had never seen an animal like this, not even in books or movies. Its body was light and fluffy, but somehow firm

to the touch. For the first time, he accepted that this thing was tangible and real.

The creature smiled and jumped off Daxton's shoulder with its wings outstretched. After gliding down to the desk, it paced around, sniffing the satchel.

"Whatever you are, you need a name." Daxton thought for a moment. "Vapor?"

The creature shook its head.

"You're right," Daxton agreed. "You're way too pretty for a name like that. In fact, you're so pretty you must be a girl. Steam?"

With a huff, the creature rolled its eyes and tilted its little head up to blow softly.

"Hmm. What about Wind?"

The little creature pranced around, letting clouds escape her paws.

"Ah, so Puffy, then?" Daxton asked.

Daxton watched for a moment as the clouds formed under his new ship. The boat began to move, its hull scraping lightly against the wooden desktop. The clouds lifting it up.

This is totally a dream. "You can make it fly?" Daxton said, watching it float on clouds.

The creature whipped its white tail, causing a soft breeze to inflate the sails.

It was at that moment that the perfect name for his new creature formed in his head. "Brea," he said.

The little creature lowered the boat and ran through the steering wheel to then explore the lower deck.

Daxton laughed, watching her enjoy the vessel.

Brea returned above deck and eyed a button on Daxton's shirt. With her claws flat out and legs bent like a cat, Brea launched forward, landing right on her target. She crawled up to his shoulder, jumping for joy before launching herself around his head.

"Are you hungry?"

What does she eat anyway, bugs?

Brea nodded as a piece of chocolate from Daxton's stash lifted into the air, floating to her. She grinned big, nibbling the chocolate.

"Well, at least you're not trying to eat my fingers." He said, moving his hand to pet her.

Brea purred at his touch, swaying her tail happily as she finished her chocolate.

Tiffany poked her head through the door. "What was that sound? Did something break?" Her sweet voice was full of curiosity.

Daxton whirled around. The blonde-haired girl was holding a large pink case with the words 'Tiffany Taylor's Sewing Kit' glued onto it in big glittery letters. He rolled his eyes when he saw it.

Of course, she's bringing her sewing kit. She refused to leave the house without it.

"What sound?" he asked nervously, looking for Brea with the intent to hide her, but could not find her anywhere. "I uh, didn't hear anything," he responded as his eyes darted around the room.

"And what are you doing in my room anyway? You know there's a 'No Girls Allowed' sign on the door."

Tiffany backed out of the room. "Whatever. You sure have been acting strange lately," she retorted, leaving.

"Brea," Daxton whispered, looking around for her. He rubbed his head and thought.

I know I'm not losing my mind, although after what just happened, maybe I am.

He walked around the room while clapping his hand and calling Brea's name while imagining how strange he must have looked. Daxton looked under his bed, behind the bookcase, and even looked through his drawers. He moved onto the small closet and shuffled clothing about while calling Brea. A sock Daxton smacked him in the face, causing him to jump a bit.

His drawers began to open and close. In a slight panic, fearing Tiffany would hear and come back, Daxton watched the chaos grow in his room. Finally, he spotted Brea sitting on a cloud over by the window, her tail moving back and forth causing things in his room to animate. Daxton jumped up and caught a sock in the air over his head and shoved it in a drawer before quickly pushing each drawer closed. "It's going to be hard to keep you a secret if you keep this up," he said, relieved he had not imagined everything. And then Brea faded from view.

"No way," Daxton mumbled, as his brain registered what was going on.

Did she just disappear?

He stared in amazement as Brea materialized on his desk. As his hand curled around her puffy white frame, her texture changed to a mist and he could no longer see her, but something light and silky shifted in his palm. Opening his hand, he felt her hop up his arm.

"Brea?" he whispered, hardly daring to breathe.

It's strange that she can appear and disappear, but so incredibly awesome at the same time.

"Are you there?" He shook his head a bit knowing that if anyone had seen him it would be a one-way ticket to the crazy house for sure. Daxton looked over to make sure his bedroom door was closed. "Brea," he whispered to his cupped hand. He felt a tickling sensation beside his left ear while angling his head. Then Brea materialized on his shoulder, grinning, and wagging her tail, which made clouds appear around Daxton's head. "What else can you do?" he asked.

Brea flew around the room disappearing and reappearing. After a few moments, she yawned and appeared in Daxton's palm.

Daxton jumped at the sudden sight of her and petted her main. He had no idea how he got so lucky finding her, but he was sure glad he did.

"Daxton, it is time for dinner?" Thelma stated from the other side of the door.

"Coming," replied Daxton.

What will I do with you?

Unsure of what else to do, Daxton placed Brea in the new satchel and closed the lid. "Please behave. I will be back soon.

As he opened the door to the hall, the sweet aromas of honey-baked ham and chocolate cake filled the house. Everyone sat down to dinner at the large, ancient table. All around, there was an air of excitement, especially with what happened in the kitchen this morning. The children were to share a special meal and tomorrow the four older children were to go to camp while Elizabeth was to stay with a friend. Ms. Thelma and Mrs. Pat would enjoy a two-week vacation from at least some of their responsibilities!

After everyone finished their dinner, Thelma got up from the table and gathered the dirty dishes. Daxton handed Thelma his plate.

"Save your fork," Mrs. Pat suggested, looking over at Daxton. "You never know what comes next."

Daxton grabbed his fork from his dirty plate before Thelma took it away to the. He heard the fridge door open, or maybe it was the back porch door. Looking towards the archways in confusion, he was sure that there was nothing else left and that dinner was over, like so many things in his life. Just then, Thelma appeared in the doorway with a huge three-layered cake smothered in chocolate icing and abundantly decorated, including tiny figures of children dancing on the cake. At the top was a tiny house and a banner with the word 'HOME' written across it.

"That's a good-looking cake," remarked Brent, licking his lips as Thelma placed it on the table.

"We're just lucky I was able to gather enough ingredients from our neighbors after the first batter was ruined," she said. Carefully, Thelma then cut five pieces with a smile on her face as she plated each and passed them out. .

Across the table, Tiffany glared at her slice of cake, then at Brent's, a mischievous smile crossing her face when she noticed that Brent's piece had more frosting. Dipping her finger into Brent's slice, she pulled a glop of buttercream frosting and put it in her mouth.

"Ms. Thelma!" Brent protested. "Tiffany's eating my icing!"

"Oh, I am sorry," Tiffany replied innocently, "You can have mine."

"I wanted the white icing!" Brent fumed, huffing with so much force that his glasses fogged over as Tiffany licked her finger clean.

"If you two don't behave, I'll take your cake away," Thelma scolded. "And it's buttercream frosting, not icing."

"Yes, ma'am," Brent sighed, sitting down to eat Tiffany's original piece - simple, lackluster chocolate frosting. He snarled at her, pushing his glasses back up his nose.

Daxton laughed to himself while taking another bite of his piece.

Knowing that as soon as they all finished eating cake they would go outside for the bonfire, Daxton took his plate to the kitchen and headed upstairs. Once in his room, he opened the satchel and Brea eased out into his hand. "If you promise to stay invisible, you can come with me. The bonfire's pretty cool. Thelma always turns all the lights off, so it gets pitch black outside.

Brea flew to his shoulder and curled her tail around his neck before fading from sight.

"Bonfire!" shouted Brent from the stairs. "Daxton, come on!"

"Coming!" Daxton called out.

Outside, the children gathered around the fire pit under the old oak tree in the backyard. Isaac sat down beside Tiffany with a mischievous smile on his face.

"If you put a cricket on me, Isaac, I swear I'll make you eat it," Tiffany promised, giving him a suspicious look.

"It was Brent's idea," Isaac retorted, letting the cricket go.

"Brent!" Tiffany yelled, jumped up, and marched over to him, shaking her fist in his face.

Isaac and Elizabeth giggled, and Daxton smiled. It was nice that Tiffany was upset with someone else for a change.

Thelma walked around the bonfire, handing sparklers to each of the children. Daxton used his to write Brea's name in a shower of golden sparks across the air. The other kids doodled in the sky too, twirling their sparklers to make words and abstract designs that lit up the night.

When Daxton's sparkler went out, Pat handed him a jar. "Here. You can catch lightning bugs in this," she said, sneaking a lighter off the table and giving him a wink. "I'm going to make some lightning of my own," she informed, pulling out a handful of homemade smoke bombs from her pocket.

The shrill, scratchy chirrup of crickets sounded in the tall grass and fireflies shone brilliantly in the jars. Summer was here.

After all of the sparklers had gone out, it was time to gather around the fire. Splendid red flames mixed with profound yellows and oranges flared up into the darkness. Around the flames sat a throng of children, giggling and roasting marshmallows. The glimmer of the campfire reflected in their eyes like an animated photograph. Combined with the crackling of wood and the scent of smoke, the sight was mesmerizing.

Sometimes, it was hard for Daxton to feel like he was a part of this group. Something about him always felt different and he couldn't figure out exactly what that was. People didn't hate him, but they didn't exactly gravitate toward him either.

But on nights like this, he knew this was his family. They were all laughing and enjoying the night. Marshmallow covered Elizabeth's cheeks. Brent and Isaac chased fireflies and all of the other bugs they found. Even Tiffany couldn't find something to complain about. When he looked at everyone, he felt a connection. These were the nights he would always remember forever.

Daxton stood, remembering he had gifts he wanted to give everyone before they all left for camp in the morning. He ran to his room without saying a word, located the gifts, and ran back outside, eager to not miss anything.

"Where'd you run off to so fast?" Brent asked, pushing his glasses up.

"I have something for all of you," Daxton resounded.

One by one, he handed everyone a fork. He had one for himself as well. Everyone looked at him, and back at their fork, confused.

"Everyone, hold up your forks," Daxton ordered, raising his own. The confused looks continued. "I know tonight might be our last night together as a family for a few weeks, but I want you to save these forks."

"Why?" Tiffany asked, confusion crossing her face.

"Because the forks represent that the best is yet to come," Daxton said. "Many times, when dinner was over, Pat or Thelma would look at one of us and say, 'save your fork.' And sure enough, there was something better coming. So, when things in your life go unexpectedly, remember to save your fork and know the best is yet to come." He watched as each of them looked at their different forks and then he sat down and gazed at his own fork. He felt his palm itch again and scratched it.

"Bedtime, children," Thelma instructed in a soft tone, picking up Elizabeth. "Daxton, please put out the fire."

Daxton retrieved a shovel from the shed. He moved back to the fire pit.

Brea reappeared on Daxton's shoulder, watching his every move.

Daxton pushed the shovel into the ground and pulled up the soil, dumping it on the glowing embers of the fire, causing a thick plume of smoke with a few random embers to rise around him. Embers landed on him, causing him to jump back, but he was not harmed. After continuing to put out the fire, he stepped back and looked around to ensure the fire was completely out. As he turned towards the house, he heard an odd sound.

Crack!

Daxton looked down, thinking he had stepped on a stick, but there was only dirt and grass beneath his feet. He looked around to see if anyone else was outside, but other than Brea, he was alone. He took a step back to the fire.

Crack!

Frozen in mid-step, the sound echoed in his ears. The pendant glowed. His heart was beating faster than he knew possible. His palm began to burn.

Crack!

Daxton grabbed the pendant and studied it in his hand. It was open slightly, smoke rising from it. Carefully, he removed the pendant from his neck. As soon as it was off of his neck, it slowly opened. His eyes widened. Inside, he found a cracked red egg with a tiny, red claw poking out.

Can I really be lucky enough to get two pets in less than a day? he wondered, holding the pendant closer to his face.

The smoke touched his eyes, but he didn't care. He couldn't stop looking at the egg.

As a little red snout peeked out of the pendant, Daxton curled his fingers and toes, barely able to contain his excitement. Next came a fiery red tail, which lashed out like a whip and shattered what remained of the egg. His triangular nose was similar to Brea's, but bright red instead of purple and without a line at the top. Looking closer, Daxton saw tiny crimson and orange scales all over its small body. The creature was two and a half inches long, not counting its tail.

Charcoal-colored eyes locked onto Daxton's face.

Daxton smiled and the ball of fire jumped onto his nose and dashed up his forehead and into his hair. Daxton jerked back in fear of being burned, but although he felt some warmth, he was not harmed. The tiny inferno stroked Daxton's hair with his tail, then took flight with his little red wings.

A carefree breeze swirled around his fiery wings, at first making the flames burn brighter. A harsher gust blew the wings out, and the creature tumbled to the ground in a hot ball of charcoal and ash.

Daxton glanced at Brea on his shoulder and chuckled, realizing that she caused the wind.

The smoldering inferno sped across the yard, drawing Daxton's attention to it. With each step, it left paw prints of black soot on the ground. As his heart pounded in his chest, he watched the creature dance around, chasing its tail like a baby kitten. Stepping closer, Daxton felt the heat radiating from the creature's body and wondered if it might burn something. He knew he should be afraid, but somehow couldn't help smiling as he watched it scamper around.

Soon, the perfect name for his new pet occurred to him. "Blaze," Daxton called, and the creature stopped and pranced toward him, showering red sparks that shimmered like fireworks.

Daxton slowly approached the small creature. His blue eyes met Blaze's, hoping to earn the creature's trust by maintaining eye contact.

Blaze cocked his head as the boy moved closer.

Daxton managed to come almost close enough to touch the wary fireball. He sat down in the grass and let Blaze prance around, flicking his fiery tail and wings. Daxton glanced at Brea, who was still on his shoulder, and wondered if the two would get along. In nature, the combination of wind and fire was dangerous. It could cause forest fires or explosions. Brea did not appear unhappy to see the fire creature, so Daxton found it fitting to introduce the two. "Blaze, this is Brea."

Blaze's eyes lit up in excitement and he made little hopping motions. He was full of energy and was ready to play. Brea, however, looked at the newly hatched creature up and down and rolled her eyes slowly. She was in no mood for this little creature. She blew a little air at Blaze, like she was trying to keep him away.

"Brea, be nice," said Daxton.

Blaze crept up Daxton's arm, closer to Brea, who huffed cool air and snuggled into Daxton's neck. As Blaze continued to within a few inches of her, Brea blew a gust of air at the newcomer, causing his fiery main to erupt into a burst of flame and forcing him to tumble back down Daxton's arm.

Daxton jerked on instinct. He chided himself since he already knew Blaze would not hurt him. As he picked up Blaze, who had a big smile on his little face, Daxton's smile matched that of the creature.

This is the coolest day of my life! Even if he's a little dangerous and, uh, weird, but this is awesome.

"Look, I know we are new to each other and all, and you don't know the rules, heck I don't even know the rules cause I don't know what you are, but in that house," Daxton urged, looking between the two creatures and pointing at the house, "are two ladies who can be a bit crazy, and, well, just try not to let them know you are here. And please do not blow the house up, okay?"

Brea and Blaze both stared at Daxton with their large, round eyes. Then they looked at each other and back at Daxton with a smile.

Brea blew back Blaze's mane and ran off. Daxton couldn't help but laugh and watched as Blaze gave chase. Daxton's eyes grew wide every time the two creatures passed him, blowing hot and cool air near his face. They would zip by and chase one another, majestically soaring throughout the yard. The two creatures frolicked in the grass for several minutes until the fun was interrupted.

"Daxton, lights out," called Thelma from the house.

Daxton knew it was past bedtime. He scooped up Blaze and Brea and walked back to the orphanage, laughing. A soft glow from the windows of the house beckoned him forward. "I promise we'll play again tomorrow," he whispered. "I just have to figure out how to get you to camp without anyone noticing."

Brea grinned, faded away, and blew Daxton's hair, making Blaze sit up on his hind legs.

At least sneaking Brea in will be easy.

Daxton walked towards the house laughing. The moon, once shining and bright, all but disappeared, leaving him in complete darkness. He felt a chill creep down his spine.

Run! a voice cried out in Daxton's head. He couldn't move; his body stiff from fright.

Something crashed behind him. He willed his body to move, and slowly, he turned around to inspect it.

Nothing. No, not nothing. Nothingness. A shadow?

He took a step back as Blaze growled.

My eyes are just playing tricks on me, right? It's just the shadows.

He closed his eyes.

Brea flapped her wings, and Blaze growled once again. Daxton opened his eyes, seeing nothing but darkness, but somehow, he knew something was out there waiting for him in the shadows.

Run! the voice yelled, overpowering the other noises. This time, he was able to listen and darted back to the house, his heart beating fast.

Once inside, he slowed, realizing he was under the watchful eyes of Ms. Thelma, who was ready for bed.

"Sorry, I lost track of time," Daxton stuttered, cupping Blaze against his side. He tried to calm down and hoped Ms. Thelma wouldn't notice anything out of the ordinary.

"It's fine," Thelma responded, a smile on her face. "You don't often get time to yourself, and it is so nice out tonight. Get some sleep and make sure you wake up early enough to eat before the bus gets here. Good night."

"Night," he answered, walking as fast as he could to the stairs. His heart felt as if it was going to explode with both excitement and fear as the realization of what had just happened.

But what had just happened? He couldn't be sure, but his mind was pulling him in every direction.

It was just a trick of the eyes. As Thelma would say, too much excitement for one day. It felt so real, though. I couldn't have imagined that. Not ever.

The house was as quiet as Daxton ever remembered. The other orphans were sound asleep, and the last thing Daxton wanted to do was wake anyone. After climbing the stairs, he crept his way down the hallway. Daxton made his way to his room where he set the creatures on his bed. Moving over to his small dresser, he quickly changed, throwing his clothing on the floor. His eyes went big, seeing his blue jeans lift up and float over to the clothing basket. "All right, I could get used to this," he said, looking at Brea. With a deep breath, Daxton moved over to his bed where he rubbed Brea's soft cloud mane before moving to pet Blaze's flaming mohawk. "Today has been a very strange day," he said, looking at Brea and Blaze while replaying the events of the day in his mind.

"Do you think I uh, I am, uh, magical or something," he mumbled. "There must be a reason you guys came to me." Hearing the words out loud sounded crazy and he shook his head. "Nope." He pulled the quilt back and got into bed. "There is no such thing as magic."

Brea wagged her tail and let out a big yawn, making clouds appear and float across the room while Blaze just looked at the boy and arched his wings.

Maybe they understood him. His right palm itched again, and he gave it a good scratch.

What is going on?

He picked up Brea and then Blaze while looking into their small eyes. They didn't weigh but a pound or less, but their weight was comforting as Daxton snuggled them on his chest as he laid his head back on his pillow. The rhythm of their breathing soon matched his as they curled into one another and fell asleep.

He tossed and turned as his mind raced.

Who am I? What am I? Where did I come from?

As these troubling questions haunted him, he felt the warmth of Blaze on his chest. As strange as everything that had happened today was, he felt an odd sense of knowing that there was more; that there was a place where he belonged. Drifting off to sleep, he muttered, "Mother."

CHAPTER 3 - BLAZE

Daxton awoke to strange noises. It wasn't too unusual in this house. He rubbed his eyes and yawned, amazed at the dream he had last night. He opened his eyes and saw Brea and Blaze blowing fireballs and air balls at one another.

It wasn't a dream! They're real!

His eyes widened, realizing what Brea and Blaze were doing. He didn't know how powerful Blaze's fire was and it scared him a little. He was afraid things would catch on fire, but so far nothing had. Blaze arched his wings and blew another fireball at Brea and she blew the ball back.

"Blaze, Brea, stop that," Daxton said, jumping out of bed, careful not to add to the noise.

Tiffany is gonna hear and come snooping!

"Daxton, who are you talking to?" Pat called from the other side of the door.

"No one," Daxton responded, quickly realizing that it was going to be very hard to keep these two creatures a secret.

"Come down and eat your breakfast! It's almost time to leave," Pat said.

"Okay," Daxton yelled through the door.

"You two have to behave," he whispered, looking at Brea and Blaze.

Daxton dressed quickly. There was still so much to do before the bus got there. Moving to the desk, he made a checklist of everything he needed to bring. Brea handed him a pencil and Daxton patted her on the head with one hand while writing with the other. She moved under his hand, like she didn't want it to end.

Blaze sat on top of the book, which began to jump like a fish out of water. He flew in the air and growled at the book for a second before moving next to it.

Daxton rubbed his eyes in disbelief. Slowly he put his hand on the book. It instantly went still. The book was large and had a woven leather cover with four triangles that connected at the tip to make a large square in the center of the cover. At the top of the cover was nothing until Daxton rubbed his fingers across the triangles. Above them a word appeared in antiquate gold.

"Eldragor," Daxton read aloud. Rubbing his chin, he opened the heavy cover to the first page, which contained a single sentence written in elegant calligraphy: *When ready, knowledge will be revealed.* Suddenly the book slammed closed.

Frowning in confusion, Daxton tried to open the book again, but had no luck. He turned it over, sending a cloud of dust into the air. Daxton sneezed and the book flipped itself open. "No," he whispered, slamming the book shut. This was all becoming too much. Discovering Brea and Blaze was one thing, but a book that could move on its own was too much for him. Who knew what he would find if he looked at the pages more thoroughly? His voice trembled, "I, uh, I changed my mind!"

Against his will, the book opened again. Daxton scrambled away from it and backed against the wall where he watched in awe as the aged and yellowed pages turned on their own accord.

It's possessed by evil spirits or something.

Fear clamped down on him, making him sick to his stomach. He managed to get a grip on himself and approached the book cautiously. Once Daxton was able to get close enough, he bent down and slammed it shut again, pressing on the cover with all his weight. The book bucked and heaved beneath him before finally flinging Daxton off as it burst open again.

"This isn't happening," he muttered from the floor.

But if Brea and Blaze are real, what's happening with the book must be real too. But these kinds of things just don't happen, right? Magic like this isn't real.

"I must be dreaming. Yeah, I'm still dreaming. No more scary movies for me." Daxton pushed himself up and then shuffled over to the book. It swung up and hit him in the chest. "Ouch!" he yelped. Definitely not dreaming. Brea and Blaze made a noise like they were laughing. At least if this is all really happening, it means they're real too.

The book flipped open to a random page. There, in big letters, were the words *Eldragor, 'A Secret Society for Elementors.'*

"A Society for Elementors," he read aloud. "What is an elementor? I hate science."

He grabbed the book and tried to move it to his desk, but it stuck to his hand like glue. "Hey! Get off me!" He couldn't let go of it no matter how hard he tried.

Blaze and Brea cocked their heads, watching in confusion from their spot on the bed.

Pat's voice drifted up the stairs. "Daxton, you need to hurry! You'll miss breakfast!"

Shaking his head at the ridiculous situation, Daxton sat on the bed and used his feet to try to pry the book from his hand.

"Listen," he protested. "I need to go and…."

"Daxton, did you hear me calling you?" Pat asked, opening the door.

He tucked his hand beneath him and smiled, pretending everything was normal. "Uh, yes, ma'am. I'll be down in a minute."

"Okay," Pat said. "You need to eat so you do not get hungry on the bus."

As she left, the book flipped open again to a page with illustrations of various beasts, each one different in appearance. Some were drawn in flight, while others were shown burrowing into the ground. Others belched fire or breathed frost.

Daxton shut the book. "No," he muttered flatly. The morning had barely begun, and he was ready for the day to be over.

The book smacked him hard on the forehead. "All right!" he sputtered through gritted teeth, feeling stupid for talking to an inanimate object.

The book laid there as an eye raised up in the center. Its eyelid opened to a multi-color eyeball, then flipped to the next page.

I am going crazy!

He watched in disbelief as 'eleagons' was written in a beautiful font of twisted golden wire. "Eleagons are exceptionally uncommon elemental creatures resembling dragons," Daxton read aloud. "When they are near a pure form of their element, they grow stronger." The book slammed shut and fell from Daxton's hands.

"Eleagons," Daxton repeated slowly. He looked at Blaze and Brea. His eyes widened with realization and excitement. They were real and they had a name. "You two are eleagons." Smiling, he felt even more of a connection until he noticed his hand was glowing again. "What am I?" he asked aloud, shaking from head to toe. He had always felt different from the other orphans, but not this different.

It was exciting and scary at the same time because he was beginning to realize that this all was tied to his parents somehow. Tears stung Daxton's eyes as he was jerked back from his thoughts by Thelma's shrieking. "Bus! The bus is here! Children!"

The book slammed on his hand.

"Ouch!"

The eye Daxton had seen before was now closed and sunken into the cover. He quickly shoved the book and the eleagons into his satchel, grabbed his pendant, and ran downstairs and out the door with everyone else. He heard something hit the floor, but he didn't have time to see what it was. With his shoes untied and the satchel banging against his side, Daxton hustled from the house. Then, so fast Daxton could barely see him, Blaze zoomed out of the satchel back toward the house with Brea following him.

Daxton stopped and watched the two scampers off.

"Daxton! Get on the bus!" Tiffany shouted.

The two eleagons flew into the house. "I forgot something!" Daxton shouted and ran back inside.

This can't be happening! They're going to get seen and then who knows what would happen to them? I have to get them back before it's too late! I should have buckled the satchel. I wonder what scared them so much. Could it have been the bus?

"Daxton!" Tiffany shouted again, running towards the house to see what was wrong. "Honestly!"

Brent followed, looking curiously at Daxton.

As Daxton started up the front stairs, he heard Pat click her tongue. She was talking with someone, or something. "Well, aren't you a pretty girl? Where did you come from?"

Daxton's feet screeched to a stop. Oh no. He turned to see Pat on the couch in the parlor, turning the pages of a book. "Hello, Daxton. Aren't you supposed to be on the bus?"

"Um," mumbled Daxton. "I forgot something."

Pat smiled and returned to her book. Both Brea and Blaze were sitting on top of the pendant, which was on the floor where Daxton must have accidentally dropped it when he raced down the stairs.

Daxton grabbed the pendant and slipped it on. He quickly shoved Brea and Blaze into the satchel and closed the clasps.

"Daxton!" Tiffany yelled from the doorway.

"I found it!" Daxton proclaimed, rushing out.

"What was it?" Tiffany asked

"Daxton, Tiffany, come on!" called Brent from the front porch.

"A necklace!" Tiffany sassed, looking at it.

"It's important. Now, let's go!" Daxton asserted, now on the porch.

"It's about time," Brent said.

"What's so important about a necklace? Tiffany asked behind him.

Daxton ignored her jogging down the front steps.

The three of them ran for the bus; the bus that was no longer there.

It had left without them.

CHAPTER 4 - THE WOODS

"What are we going to do now?" Tiffany wailed. "Daxton, this is all your fault! And for what? That necklace?

"You didn't have to follow me," Daxton retorted, looking at her crossly. He felt Brent's hand pull at the pendant.

"Is it made of real gold?" Brent asked, turning the pendant in his hands

"I can't believe you made us miss the bus for a necklace!" Tiffany exclaimed.

"It could have been part of a buried treasure," Brent said, studying the necklace. "It looks very old."

"Buried treasure?" Tiffany asked, changing her tune. "Where did you find it?

Like I'm going to tell you.

Daxton ignored their questions and snatched the heavy golden pendant back from Brent's hand and slipped it under his blue shirt. "If we cut through the woods, we might be able to catch the bus," he interjected, turning around and heading for the trail behind the house.

It's none of their business where I got the pendant.

The narrow trail led through the woods to the stop sign at the end of the road about half a mile away. The bus would have to stop there. If they hurried they might be able to make it, if they were lucky.

It was a hot and humid summer day. Ducking under a few branches, all Daxton wanted to do was play with his eleagons. Tiffany and Brent were behind him talking, dragging their luggage. It wasn't long until he heard water in the distance and instantly regretted taking the shortcut.

Yeah, forgot about this.

There was a creek at least ten feet wide that they needed to cross via an old broken bridge. The only way to fully cross the creek was to get to the end of the broken bridge without falling in, and then jump from boulder to boulder.

Daxton had zero intentions of getting wet; he hated deep water. Just the thought of not being able to breathe was terrifying, and the bridge looked like it was going to fall in at any moment. He tested the first board with his foot and sure enough, the rotten board caved in around his foot, breaking off and floating downstream.

Nope!

"We can go around," Daxton said.

"And miss the bus!" Tiffany exclaimed, tightening the straps of her pink backpack. "You will not ruin my summer."

"It's not that deep, we could cross," Brent informed, adjusting his glasses.

Or drown.

Daxton had turned around to find another route when he heard the bridge creaking. He turned back around to see Tiffany making her way across the broken bridge. She had already thrown her luggage to the other side.

She's gonna fall in.

Before long, she was hopscotching from boulder to boulder until she was safe and sound on the other side.

"See, easy!" Tiffany yelled.

"Come on, we can do it," Brent said as he began to make his way across the old bridge.

Brent jumped from boulder to boulder, and Daxton memorized the ones he jumped to because he knew Brent would have jumped on the steadiest boulder and found the best path to the other side.

I can do this.

Carefully, he held his hand on the broken rail and took his first step. The bridge didn't give away like earlier but held him there. He took another big step over a place where a missing board was and could hear the water rushing below.

With a deep breath, he continued on the rickety old bridge. Very carefully, he placed one foot in front of the other. Just a few more steps and he found himself at the end, looking at the first boulder.

Too late to turn back now.

With a big jump, he made it to the first boulder and then to the second one.

So far, so good.

THE ELEAGONS AND THE ELEMENTAL RIFT

Proud of himself, he looked up, wanting Tiffany or Brent to cheer him on, but to his surprise, they were nowhere to be seen.

Why couldn't they wait?

Daxton moved from the other boulders with ease. Getting to the last boulder, he waited a moment until he spotted a good landing spot. With all his might, he sprang from the boulder and landed safely. He heaved a sigh of relief.

I am glad that's over!

Needing to catch up with Brent and Tiffany, he ran down the narrow, beaten path to the edge of the tree line. He suddenly felt an icy chill moving through him. Ahead, amongst the shadows, he made out Tiffany and Brent lying motionless.

Are they dead?

Suddenly the shadows moved as though they were alive.

Are those red eyes in the shadows? Daxton wondered.

Although Daxton was now terrified and he wanted to run, he could not leave his friends.

I must save them!

He started to run to his friends, but the shadows now move between him and them.

Brea flew out of the satchel to the top of Daxton's hand. His left palm burned, but he couldn't get distracted by that now. Brea blew hard, forcing the shadows across the clearing. Daxton rushed to his friends where he touched their cold hands.

Blaze joined in and made a wall of flame between Daxton and the shadows, which had recovered and were moving back across the clearing. Daxton had no idea Blaze could do something like that, but he didn't have time to think about it. *I have to do something quickly.* He started chest compressions on Tiffany like he had seen on tv.

Please, let this work!

Nothing happened.

Looking up, Daxton saw that the shadows were now floating over the wall of fire. "Blaze! More! I need more fire!" Daxton pleaded, desperately.

Blaze made the fire larger, but not by much. The little fire creature seemed exhausted.

Brea flapped her cloud wings and took in a huge breath. Her front paws pulled back, her tail arched, and she blew a mighty wind that fed the wall of flames, which ate the air like it was starving, growing higher and higher. The intensified fire lept and burned the shadows, which pulled back behind the wall..

Daxton saw his eleagons, their little bodies giving all their power to protect them, but Daxton knew it was not enough.

The shadow now moved through the trees and around behind Daxton. The eleagons were now spent, and Daxton had no defense. Nothing stood between his friends and the shadow, except Daxton.

Daxton realized that the shadow was in the shape of some sort of feline creature, like a giant black panther. Somehow that made Daxton less afraid. It at least now had a form.

Maybe if it has a form it can be defeated.

Quickly, he stepped forward to meet the shadow beast. With a growl, the shadow beast lept at Daxton, who closed his eyes and stretched his arms out towards it. Pain from his palm overcame him as he felt a force flow through and out of his body towards the beast.

When Daxton opened his eyes, the shadow beast was gone, but a woman was walking towards him. She was tall and slender with a peach complexion and dark blue eyes. Her hair was the color of chestnut and fitted in a tight bun with a metal, golden feather. She wore soft eggplant-colored leather gloves that matched her high calf boots and long trench coat. Floating at her side was an oversized, multi-colored purple carpet bag that had lots of different golden triangles on it.

With a stern but confident look, she spoke, "Well, that was certainly impressive."

What?

"Who are you?" Daxton asked. It seemed like a good starting point.

"My name is Madame Theresa Thorten. Are they hurt?" Theresa asked, looking at the two other children.

They're not moving; of course they're hurt.

Daxton said nothing, watching her retrieve from her bag two tiny, corked glass tubes, each filled with periwinkle colored liquid. A flick of her wrist was all it took for the tubes to glow and the corks to pop off. She plucked a strand of Tiffany's and Brent's hair, which she then released into the air that then blew them into the tubes.

The hairs sizzled, transforming the periwinkle liquids to the faintest tinge of black in seconds. "Negments," Madame Theresa huffed. "Barely any elemental power." She paused and looked down at them. "Now, what am I going to do with these two?" she asked, returning the tubes to her bag.

Nothing!

Daxton watched her take a very deliberate step backward. She was studying the children laying on the ground. With a flick of her index finger, her carpet bag opened and out came a couple of puffs of dust followed by an old, worn pamphlet. Daxton read the title as it flew to her hand, *How to Handle a Negment*.

He watched her thumb through it before she threw it back in her bag.

"What are you doing with the Negments? Explain your reasoning this instant! Did you tell them our secrets! You could be banned for this!" Madame Theresa asked, looking at him.

Does this woman speak English?

Daxton saw the confusion on her face. She straightened her posture and looked around. "Do you know what that was?"

"No," Daxton replied.

"Maybe you haven't learned it, or you've been living under a rock," Theresa said.

"Learned what?" Daxton asked.

"That there was a vorous beast," Madame Theresa responded loudly. "It's an elemental creature made from darkness."

"Made from darkness? That's not a thing." Daxton retorted.

"This is why I quit teaching! They begged me to come back! I should have said no," Theresa related.

"Uh?" Daxton muttered.

"Darkness!" Theresa fussed. "You should at least know what that is."

If you say so.

"Like a shadow," responded Daxton.

"Darkness is similar to shadow, but not the same."

"All right, well this has been fun," Daxton mused, still unsure of this stranger.

Theresa took out her pocket watch and flipped the lid open to check the time. "I don't have time for this! Either you are playing a game, or you have lost your mind," she said, looking at the two still laying on the ground. "They should've woken up by now."

"You think?" Daxton said.

"Don't get an attitude! I can still see them breathing. Negments in the Normal Lands are not supposed to be affected by vorous beasts. I've been hunting that one for weeks."

"Hunting?" Daxton asked.

"Yes, hunting," Theresa gloated, looking at him closely. "How did you find it?"

"Find it?" Daxton asked. "It found us."

Who in their right mind would go looking for that thing?

Theresa took out what looked like a magnifying glass with many shades of glass and gears from her coat pocket. She flipped the outside, turning the gears while holding the antique handle to scan Tiffany and Brent. The lens changed from clear to a murky green.

"That beast has infected this girl and that boy there. It's odd it would hunt Negments."

"Why is it here? Are there more?" Daxton asked.

"When they need easy prey, they come here," Madame Theresa informed. "Vorous beasts don't attack Negments; they feed off the elemental energy that is left behind. A beast as powerful as that would have more satisfaction from a shadow of a tree than it would from a Negment, yet it did something to them."

Tiffany and Brent started to move, and their skin color returned to normal.

"What happened? Who are you?" Tiffany asked, rubbing her head.

"Wait, you said they're infected?" Daxton asked, talking over Tiffany.

"Yes, infected. The vorous beast can drain elemental energy, and in its place leave an infection. I don't know the specifics as that is not my specialty. They will need to drink a special brewtion to take away the infection."

Daxton watched her reach inside the pocket of her robe and removed two small glass vials, each the size of a child's pinkie. The vials shimmered, and round shapes moved through the purple and silver liquid inside.

"What are those?" Tiffany asked suspiciously as she continued to gain her strength.

Madame Theresa ignored her. "Each of you, drink one of these. It should eliminate the infection of shadow."

"Is it safe?" Brent asked.

"I wouldn't drink that," stated Daxton. "We've always been told not to take things from strangers."

And she clearly isn't a normal stranger.

Madame Theresa sighed, pulling out another vial. She drank it quickly. "See? Perfectly safe. You need to get rid of this infection."

"Are you sure this will cure the infection?" Brent asked, pulling off the cork and then sniffing the liquid.

"Yes," Theresa answered, growing annoyed with them.

"It's not bad tasting. Like caraway seeds and cotton candy. Strange, but not bad," Brent said.

"Daxton, can you tell us who this is?" Tiffany asked, drinking hers.

I know just as much as you.

"No, he cannot," Theresa countered.

"Why not?" Tiffany asked.

"Our kind doesn't share secrets," Madame Theresa explained, sighing.

What does she mean? Our kind?

"Why?" Tiffany inquired, finishing the liquid. "Are you magical?"

"Magic?" Madame Theresa repeated, sneering at him. "That word is for people who don't know what they're doing. That is a brewtion made from elemental alchemy, the interaction of physical and essential properties of nature. It is not magic. I don't have time for your nonsense, young lady," Theresa scolded. She moved her magnifying glass again over Tiffany and Brent.

"Daxton, what is going on?" Tiffany asked.

Daxton felt his satchel move and before he could close it, Brea snuck out, followed by Blaze.

When did they get in my satchel? Did I pass out also?

"What? How?" Madame Theresa gasped, using the magnifying glass to examine Brea and Blaze. She flipped it a few times to obtain focus.

Daxton gulped as he watched Brea climb up his torso to settle onto his left shoulder, followed by Blaze, who curled up on his right shoulder.

"How did you get those?" Madame Theresa demanded.

Daxton didn't have an answer that he wanted to give. He knew by the look on her face that they must be important to this woman and Daxton wasn't willing to give them up.

"What?" Daxton asked.

Please don't say 'eleagons.' Please don't say 'eleagons.'

"Those eleagons!"

Blast! She said it.

An odd wave of emotion swept through Daxton.

"Lady," Tiffany said. "We need to take you to a zoo so you can learn all about animals. Those are," She took a breath, looking at the creatures on Daxton's shoulder. "Birds?"

"Answer me and answer me now!" Theresa demanded.

"I hatched them," Daxton pronounced.

"And I pulled a sword out of a broom. Let's not lie to each other.

We are far past lies and secrets here."

"I'm not lying!"

Madame Theresa snorted at his answer. "Tell me your name," she demanded.

Brea and Blaze flew around Daxton's head, almost protectively.

"Daxton," Daxton answered.

"Daxton what?" Theresa asked, staring intently at the eleagons.

"Tanner," Daxton answered.

Theresa grabbed his left hand, quickly turning it over to reveal the welt mark on his palm. "An air array. Why are you not in Eldragor?"

Eldragor? What?

Daxton was so stunned he could barely understand what Madame Theresa was saying. Questions flooded his mind. Eldragor? There's really an Eldragor?

I might be able to learn more about my eleagons in Eldragor. What if I never get another chance to find out where I belong?

"Did you say my element is a-air?" Daxton stuttered, almost involuntarily.

"Yes, air by the looks of it," Theresa repeated. "You will start off in my Society, Aero, but we won't be certain of anything until the ceremony."

By the looks of it?

"Air?" Daxton asked.

"Did the eleagons help you chase off the vorous beast?" Theresa asked.

"What?" Daxton asked.

Is she saying I did that? I thought she did that.

"It all makes sense now. The vorous beast didn't want the Negments; it wanted to absorb the eleagons," Theresa said, shaking her head while scanning Tiffany and Brent again. Still, the glass remained murky green.

Daxton lifted Brea and then Blaze from his shoulders, and put them both back into the satchel, closing it and tightening the clasps.

"Obviously, you know absolutely nothing," Theresa stated. "How you hatched two pure eleagons is beyond me, but you will want to keep them hidden as much as possible, especially once I get you to Eldragor."

"Why?" Tiffany asked, tilting her head.

Theresa looked between the three a moment before shifting her weight. Daxton didn't know if she was going to start shooting fireballs so he gulped and pulled the leather strap of his satchel over his shoulder, but Brent spoke before Theresa could.

"Until they know that Daxton is their dad," Brent answered.

"Yes, until they know that," Theresa agreed.

She's lying, but why? And why are Brent and Tiffany not freaking out?

Theresa took the magnifying glass and waved it over Brent then Tiffany yet again, still the glass went from clear to murky green.

"Is there a problem?" Brent asked, pushing up his glasses again.

"Yes, you two are still infected and I am not sure why. When the vorous beast attacked you, did you see anything?"

"No," they both answered.

"The brewtion should have worked, but it still shows you are infected. I can't just leave you two here," Madame Theresa paused, "for if I did, you would be dead in a month at most two."

"What do you mean dead?" Tiffany demanded.

"Dead? Like dead-dead?" Brent asked.

"Yes, dead," Theresa grunted. Motioning to Tiffany and Brent, she demanded, "Let me see your palms"

Daxton watched them both turn their palms over like they were waiting for candy.

"You don't even have arrays trying to break free." Theresa stated. "You will have no way to defend yourself from another attack or from the infection." Theresa paused, walking on air back and forth, shaking her head, and mumbling to herself. After a few moments, she looked between Tiffany and Brent. "Well then, that's settled. I do not have time to sort this all out. All three of you shall come with me to Eldragor. I will sort it out when we get there. I will be your sponsor."

All three children looked nervous.

Is this really happening? Attacked by a shadow beast? Infected? This woman? This can't be real.

"Brent, Tiffany, you will have to promise to keep Eldragor societies' secrets until you are well," Theresa said.

"I promise," Tiffany vowed, her voice trembling.

"I promise too," Brent said.

"If you ever break this promise, bad things will happen," Madame Theresa said. "Now give me your palms again."

Daxton looked on as Tiffany and Brent raised and turned their palms over. Theresa placed hers on top of their blank palms, imprinting the air symbol on the inside of their palms.

"That triangle is like a cut. It is only temporary. This symbol will allow you to pass through basic air barriers until you are well. Once it fades, so will everything you have learned with it. Do you understand?"

"Yeah!" Tiffany and Brent answered at the same time.

"All right then, let's go," Madame Theresa ordered.

"One problem. How are we all going to get there?" Brent asked.

"We fly of course," Madame Theresa responded, tapping her finger in mid-air, signaling for her carpet bag. She held her forefinger and thumb in the air to unzip the carpet bag. With a double tap of her finger, out popped a basket.

"Um, it's kinda small?" Tiffany said.

"How are we going to travel with this?" Brent asked. "Where's the rest of it?"

"Oh, you Negments cannot see anything," Madame Theresa snapped.

"There is no balloon," Brent observed.

Madame Theresa dug in the carpet bag until she found what she was looking for. With a flick of her hand, a large purple nylon sheet expanded like a balloon, reaching high for the sky. The basket grew ten times its size as the ropes began to attach to it.

A hot air balloon? No way!

"Climb in and hurry up!"

"Yay! Magic!" squealed Tiffany, climbing in.

"It is not magic," Madame Theresa corrected in a harsh tone.

"Seems like magic," Brent hypothesized.

"We don't use sticks for power or fly on brooms." Madame Theresa said, rolling her eyes.

"What is this thing called?" Daxton asked.

"It's a bket," Madame Theresa responded, tapping her heels together to make a cloud staircase. The side of the bket lowered. "It's an air elemental artifact," she said, getting it. "It is equipped with the light factors that will hide us from any other Negments we encounter on our way to the LEAF. I use it when I need to travel so I can carry things. Or people, if I must."

"Bee-ket," Tiffany pronounced. "That's a funny word. What's a Negment?"

"A person from the Normal Lands. One who can neither sense nor use the elements," Madame Theresa responded in frustration. "As I stated before, we are short on time so please stop talking and just hold on. I was not expecting to take more than two on this bket. No more questions for three minutes," she huffed, opening a compartment to grab a pair of goggles and a map.

"What about our luggage?" Tiffany asked.

"You Negments and your silly never-ending things," Madame Theresa complained.

She waved her hand, causing more strings to reach out from the basket and grab their luggage.

Daxton smiled, knowing this was going to be a summer he would never forget. He slowly touched the triangle in the center of his palm, now aware he was truly different; maybe Tiffany and Brent were too.

CHAPTER 5 - ELDRAGOR

Lurching forward through the air on the bket, Daxton couldn't believe this was real. He had never even been on an airplane before, let alone anything like this. As high up in the air as he had ever been in his life, he wasn't sure if he was supposed to be excited or terrified at this new experience. Instead of picking one, he chose both.

Daxton watched Theresa as the round, glowing purple pattern lifted off her palm. It was an intricate pattern of lines, angles, circles, triangles, and more. With a slight move of her fingers, the circle shifted, directing the air.

In the center of her palm was something Daxton recognized, the burn mark. He stared at hers before touching his own.

Could I really be an elementor? I have to find out.

"What is that?" Daxton asked, pointing at Theresa's palm.

"What is what? This!" Madame Theresa asked, arching her eyebrows, and motioning her palm upward. "My array?"

That was no help!

Daxton looked at her in confusion. This was the first time he really felt dumb. How was he going to fit in?

"You truly don't know what it is? It controls the air," she said proudly, watching the purple patterns on her palm spin like a wildfire burning out of control.

"Yours will come in fully, and in time you will be able to advance yours and add sub elements to it," Madame Theresa answered.

Daxton nodded and looked down.

"I know this is a lot, but trust me, it will be easy. Besides, you forced away a vorous beast." Madame Theresa shrugged her shoulders. "You have power of some sort."

Daxton smiled and checked his satchel to find his two eleagons fast asleep. He didn't realize they were so strong.

Should I tell Madame Theresa that the eleagons forced the beast away while I just stood there with my eyes closed?

"Daxton, your satchel is very nice," Madame Theresa said, eyeing it. "Where did you get it?"

Great, something else she might want.

"I needed something for summer camp and I sorta found this in the closet."

"Do you know what it is?" Madame Theresa asked.

"A satchel?" Daxton answered.

"Well, yes but do you know anything else?" Madame Theresa questioned, leaning forward.

"No?" Daxton said.

"It's a holding satchel, like my carpet bag. The threads have been etched using elemental power. It will hold more than it should."

"Oh," Daxton replied, his eyes growing wide.

"Yes," Madame Theresa said.

"That's incredible, I was wondering how everything seemed to fit," Daxton answered.

"Well, now you know," Madame Theresa said, "I would recognize that tailor anywhere; fine work she does. It's very special and a mystery how it came to be in your home and not in the LEAF." She arched her eyebrows.

"What's the LEAF?" Daxton asked, getting tired of her saying things like was supposed to know what she meant.

"The LEAF is an anagram of Liquid, Earth, Air, and Fire. It is the four elemental islands. Eldragor is the building where you and your friends will learn and live for the next eight weeks."

"Eight weeks? What are we to tell Mrs. Pat and Ms. Thelma?" Tiffany asked.

"What do you mean?" Madame Theresa asked, looking at Tiffany, confused.

"They think we're at summer camp," answered Tiffany.

"What is summer camp?" Madame Theresa questioned.

"A place where kids go during the summer," Tiffany stated. "I swim all the time, unlike Daxton, who hangs out under trees."

"You will send them an obble telling them you are having a wonderful time at summer camp," Madame said. "They can't know you're here."

"What's an obble?" Asked Daxton.

"A message carrier," Madame Theresa said. "Each element has its own form of communication; the Aero Society's is an obble."

"We don't have those down in Georgia," Brent said.

"What do you have?" Madame Theresa asked.

"Mail, email," Tiffany answered.

Daxton laughed, "Those two have no idea how to use email."

"All right, I will study this mail you speak of and make sure they get them. If there comes a time to tell them more, I will address that issue then. I have enough for now," Madame Theresa said

"How long is this going to take, anyway?" Brent asked, pressing his glasses back

"We will get there when we get there," Madame Theresa responded.

Eventually, instead of seeing the blue sky sprinkled with clouds, a bright, great mass appeared. It wasn't just some land, though. It floated in the air. All on its own! Daxton blinked a few times, but the view didn't change. They were steadily approaching something that shouldn't have been real. Amazement coursed through him as he took everything in. There was a mountain so huge it looked like its own planet floating in front of him.

Is it covered in green fur?

When he looked harder, he realized it wasn't fur, but trees! The trees, which would have looked large up close, looked like saplings as they covered the sides of this humongous mountain. There was also a waterfall; a raging torrent of water so bright Daxton was sure it would glow in the dark at night.

This place is truly special.

On a plateau at the top of a mountain sat a castle, much like the ones Daxton had seen in picture books and in fairy tales when he was younger. Each corner had a tower, and in the center was a huge dome that looked like crystal or glass. Beyond the castle was a large plain that ran to a forest as dark as night.

The bket changed course as Madame Theresa held out her hand, adjusting her air array. They swooped around the mountain and saw an entry point in the center of each of the four walls. A road led down the mountain, winding back and forth between rocks and trees. It was beautiful, but there were also signs of destruction: bare places on the mountain with broken columns and walls; areas where nothing grew; and on the castle itself were mismatched stones and big cracks everywhere. Daxton couldn't imagine what would have caused this.

"There used to be so much more here," Madame Theresa said. "The Dome has been repaired and the walls rebuilt, but it's nothing like it once was. It was almost a city here, and now look."

"What happened?" Daxton asked, but Madame Theresa focused on the glowing purple lines radiating out of her palm, bringing the bket near one of the towers. Four purple flags flew from the corners of the tower, each bearing a gold triangle.

The bket landed in front of a set of doors with a thud.

"Get out or get sucked into my carpet bag," Madame Theresa said.

Daxton jumped out and landed on the rocky ground. Looking around him, he saw large cracks embedded deep into the ground around him. The air was musky, and the sun was setting. He heard Madame Theresa behind him and saw the bket zip down to nothing and back into the carpet bag, closing with a snap. Madame Theresa picked it up and strode to the door. After picking up their things, Brent and Tiffany hurried to keep up with her, while Daxton took a moment to take in the scenery.

"Tiffany, Brent," Theresa said. "I will have someone make a special brewtion called antiium that you will have to take every fourth day. If you develop any other symptoms, please let me know."

"Yes, ma'am," Brent said.

"What kind of symptoms?" Tiffany asked.

"You will know," Madame Theresa said.

"You better catch up," an eerie, deep voice cracked from behind Daxton.

Daxton froze, jerking his head around just in time to see an old man with a humped back, a long-crooked nose, a bald head, and large, dark eyes surrounded by skin as worn as leather. He had as many warts as a toad. Daxton pulled his satchel over his shoulder and looked at the old man a bit more. Mud covered his tattered brown coat and pants as well as his bare feet, which were gnarled, causing a limp. The man pulled a seed out of a sack that was around his waist, dropped the seed onto the ground, and used his big toe to plant the seed in the ground. He took a needle out of his pocket and pricked his finger, letting the blood drip onto the soil.

"Do what?" Daxton asked, watching the man plant another seed with his toe and repeat the needle prick.

This place is weird.

Daxton turned and walked for a moment before looking back to the man again, but he was gone.

"Daxton, do please leave Sengal alone; he has lots of work to do," called out Theresa.

Shrugging his shoulders, Daxton moved over to the others who were standing on a set of cracked and broken stone stairs that led upward to a massive pair of wood doors.

"Welcome to Eldragor," Madame Theresa spoke proudly, opening the large oak doors, "This is the Aeroious Tower."

Entering, Daxton breathed in the musky air and saw a giant hall ahead. Daxton wanted to do nothing more than explore the castle, but he was pretty sure that Madame Theresa would just leave them behind if he didn't keep up.

I'll have time for exploring later.

Brent had already started exploring, Daxton realized as he saw that his friend was holding a plant that had been outside on the stone steps. It started growing larger and larger, a mass of roots twisting around Brent's arm. Brent dropped the plant, and its roots dug into the cracks on the floor. Daxton's eyes grew wide.

Theresa, with a flick of her array, made the whole plant shrivel. Brent just looked on in amazement.

"The kur plant can be very dangerous, but you look unharmed. I wish you had seen this all before the Rift. It was a sight to behold," Theresa said. "But there are some things that not even we elementors can fix."

CHAPTER 6 - THE BASICS

Madame Theresa's shoulders slumped as she looked around the entrance hall. Frowning, her gaze lingered on torn tapestries, cracked tiles, and glass bulbs that were stubbornly dark. A few other bulbs glowed with a soft, pure white light.

Daxton expected her to march off, but she lingered for a moment, putting a hand on one of the gold picture frames. "Being selected by the quill is a great honor. It means that you have been selected to learn the secrets of the elements. It used to be a very competitive process to even go before the quill to be accepted, but now we are willing to take anyone with an ounce of power." She stared at Brent and Tiffany, a sour look on her face. "Or in your case, if the vorous beast wanted to hunt you."

"Thanks for that," Tiffany said, looking at Brent and Daxton.

"Yeah," Brent chimed in.

"There are too many dangers for Negments, or late bloomers, or whatever you two are. You've already encountered the kur plant. Even rain can be deadly here. And that's saying nothing about the windstorms that pick you up and drag you over cliffs, or the death-willow trees, or the ghouls, or a hundred other things." She sighed. "A few things need to be done before you go to the ceremony," Madame Theresa said.

"Ceremony?" asked Tiffany. Her eyes grew wide.

"Not for you two, just for Daxton. Each promising elementor with an array has their power evaluated," Madame Theresa said. "Daxton, as you study, you may complete a few basic levels of your acumen. If you don't pass your classes and complete any levels before the end of the summer, you will have to leave here and you will never be able to return."

Never return?

"Brent and Tiffany, your cover story, until I find a cure, is that you are visiting from a private tutor in the Normal Lands. When the ceremony starts, you will go out with the other Aero hopefuls, but then you will stay with me, okay?" Theresa turned to Daxton. "Now, Daxton, why were you in the Normal Lands? Did your parents bring you there to escape the Rift?"

This question silenced Daxton. He stood there, his face growing hot.

How am I supposed to tell her that my parents gave me up? How do I say that Ms. Pat found me with the roses, and I have no idea who my family is? And what is a Rift?

"What?" Tiffany retorted. "Mrs. Fancy Pants, we don't have parents! We are orphans, if you must put a title on us." Tiffany smiled and stared at Theresa. "Do you know what that means? That means that our parents didn't want us for one reason or another and just left us. You can ask all the questions you want about our parents," she turned on her foot, "but the only answer you will ever get is nothing! To us, our parents are dead!"

"No parents?"

"None!"

"Who looks after you?

"Thelma and Pat Jenkins."

"All right then. We don't usually get students without parents here, so this will be new for all of us. Maybe we can all learn something after the ceremony places Daxton in his Society."

"Will Brent and I be with you then? Since you are our sponsor?" Tiffany asked.

"Correct. Enrollment in my society is sparse and we need all we can get, even if you are infected," she whispered.

"Will we be elementors?" Tiffany inquired.

"If the array I imprinted on you works, then you will be at least temporarily," Madame Theresa said. "Only time will tell. The first step is to get rid of your infection."

"Will I be able to fly on a broom or make a love potion?" Tiffany asked, smiling.

Madame Theresa gave her a pitying look. "Why on earth would you want to fly on a broom? What are the Negments teaching you? And what is a love potion?"

"If this works, will they be able to defend themselves against the beast?" Daxton asked.

"No," Theresa said.

"What do you mean no?" Tiffany asked, looking like she was about to stomp her foot on the ground.

"Just that it takes a lot of power and years of practice before one could ward one off. No, I will try to learn why the beasts are attacking Negments or late bloomers, or whatever you two are. We will see if there is something I or any of the governesses can do. Until then, we will just make the best of it."

Is any of this really happening?

"Hold still," Theresa said, opening her carpetbag. With a snap of her fingers, three black robes floated up and around each of the children.

Daxton felt the heaviness of the robe as it slipped on over his shoulders.

At least it fits.

"A perfect fit! The ceremony will start soon," Madame Theresa said.

Daxton was thankful to have something signifying he belonged here. At least he might be able to blend in a little better. Slowly, he patted the fine material of the robe. A powerful feeling moved through him while fastening the last button at his neck. Daxton smiled with pride as he walked toward his unknown future.

A group of small, multicolored orbs of elemental energy moved toward them down the hallway. Each one had either one or two eyes that looked back and forth as they moved. They were each about six inches high and different from one another. A sphere of fire rolled along the stone floor, its eyes frowning with concentration. Five blue watery globules bounced by, making little squishy noises.

Green ones rolled, leaving leaves along the way. Then an almost translucent globe of purple and silver floated right past Daxton and stopped beside Madame Theresa. Its arms popped out, holding a small teacup of tea.

"These are bubbits," explained Madame Theresa, taking the teacup. "Thank you," she added gratefully. "Peppermint tea is the best."

The bubbit turned a little pink before floating away. Brea and Blaze popped their little heads out of the side of Daxton's satchel. When they saw the green bubbit, their eyes went wide and they squirmed out the side, arching their wings to give the little earth bubbit a chase before Daxton realized what was happening.

"Hey, come back here!" Daxton called.

When they heard Daxton's voice, they slowly flew back to him with big puppy eyes. He pointed to the satchel.

Brea let out a little dark cloud as her tail closed the flap of the satchel.

Daxton rolled his eyes when their weight shifted in the satchel. He knew they wanted to play, but this wasn't the time. As a precaution, he placed the satchel under his robe and was surprised when he saw it was not noticeable.

One of the green, leaf bubbits rolled by and Tiffany crouched down to watch. "I want one of each," she said, reaching out and trying to scoop it up, but the odd creature struggled away.

"Don't do that," Madame Theresa scolded. "They're not pets. Each bubbit serves its own element. Among other things, they help keep the floors tidy."

A purple bubbit swirled around Daxton's head, making little noises.

"It wants to know if you want some tea," said Madame Theresa, nodding her head toward the bubbit.

"Thanks, but I'm good," Daxton said.

A little silver one landed on Daxton's robe and sniffed around his collar. Daxton scooped it up and his fingers sunk a little into the airy material. "It's like picking up a little piece of mud," he said in surprise.

The bubbit giggled and rolled around on his hand, then flapped its little silver wings, and rejoined the others.

"I love this earthy-looking one," Brent said, reaching down to pick up one of the three bubbits stacked on top of each other, but they separated and bounced away from his hand.

"Teachers' rooms are off the main chamber on the first and second floors. For now, the Aero Society will be your home as an Aeroious elementor, so remember everything I've said. The common area under the main dome is for all students and staff. We share it among all the elements," Madame Theresa said.

They exited through a door partially covered with a shimmering purple glow and what they saw was so amazing that even Madame Theresa had to pause for a moment to admire it.

"The Sky Dome," she said.

Directly in front of them was a grand staircase made of clouds; not stone steps decorated to look like clouds, but literal clouds that moved a little, as if an invisible breeze was blowing across them. The air had a light scent of lavender.

The other three corners of the massive room, far off in the distance, also had fantastical staircases: one that looked like hot lava flowing in the shapes of stairs; another was a cascading waterfall; and the last was made of living trees, its hanging roots decorated with sparkling bits of polished stone. At the top of each set of stairs was a banner on the wall with the symbols and colors of the corresponding element.

Above them was a portion of the massive glass dome Daxton had seen as they first arrived. It appeared to not only cover this large chamber but extended over surrounding rooms as well.

Also on the walls were old portraits in gold frames; people from history and of great significance. These were people who were born knowing their families, unlike Daxton. If his parents came from here, and if this is where he was supposed to belong, why had they left him in the Normal Lands for so long?

Maybe I don't belong here. What if I have no powers at all?

Suddenly he heard a woman's sad voice.

Daxton. You must leave this place.

CHAPTER 7 - AEROIOUS

Daxton whipped his head around, trying to find the origin of the voice.

"Daxton, are you all right?" Madame Theresa asked, raising a brow.

"I'm fine," Daxton said.

Where did that voice come from?

A large bubble floated into the hall and stopped right in front of Daxton and then popped. "We have just under an hour until the Worthiness Ceremony," echoed a woman's voice.

"What was that?" asked Brent with his voice getting louder at every word.

"Those are obbles," Theresa said.

Floating messages.

"Del," Theresa called out to a girl that was coming down the waterfall stairs.

"Yes, Madame Theresa?" Del said.

Daxton nodded as the girl walked over. The first thing he noticed about her was her sapphire blue eyes that matched her pearl-studded robe. Seashells were intertwined in her silver braids.

"Del, these are new students who need to be taken to the Aeroious section at the Worthiness Ceremony. Please escort them for me. I have to get something prepared for them."

"Of course, Madame Theresa," Del said, fixing her silver hair.

Madame Theresa nodded at them, then hurried across the floor of the Sky Dome.

"My name is Del Mooney. I'm an Aquaious elementor."

"N–Nice to meet you!" Brent said, grabbing her hand and shaking it. "This is Daxton and that is Tiffany."

"And the boy shaking your hand? We call him Brent," Tiffany said, rolling her eyes.

Del pulled her small hand back and folded her hands together with a small smile on her ivory face. "Nice to meet you. Follow me."

"What is an Aquaious elementor?" Brent asked when they started moving.

Del looked at him with raised eyebrows.

"Well, aqua means water," she said.

Daxton could tell that blending in was going to be very hard. There was so much that they didn't know. He decided to roll with it and spoke, "Oh, he must have misunderstood you. Of course, we know what an Aquaious elementor is."

"Great!" Del said, offering up a smile.

Daxton rolled his eyes. *This is going to be hard.*

They didn't have that far to go until they reached the south side of the Sky Dome and then through another set of large doors to the outside. Once outside, they followed Del as they passed pools of varying types of water: blue water, freshwater, seawater, and little ponds containing water statues and floating plants. They turned and walked to an area with broken pillars and overgrown vines.

"I wish they would get rid of these stupid remnants of the Rift," Del said.

"The what?" Daxton asked, looking at the broken pillars.

"Never mind," Del responded quickly, something catching her eye.

A blue obble arrived.

"I told you I saw it active," proclaimed a voice from the obble as it burst.

"Excuse me a moment," Del said, looking at the three nervously.

Daxton watched as Del raised her hands, made a circle with her two index fingers, and slowly blew in the center. A shiny bubble formed out the other side. Just before Del closed her fingers together, it popped.

"Obbles are very easy to create once you get the hang of it," Del said with a smile. "I just have a lot on my mind this evening and nothing is easy when one is worried about something," she said as another popped.

Daxton heard footsteps behind him. He turned and looked at a girl approaching with dark skin that contrasted with her short, white hair and bright smile. Her hair was spiked in the front, and she was taller than Del, but not by much. She was wearing a very detailed robe in various shades of blue. The fabric was covered in items from the sea such as coral and seashells. Her seemingly perfect face had drops of water, and pearls hung around her neck. Daxton didn't know if this was normal or if this particular girl just really loved the sea.

"Electra, it is so good to see you!" Del squealed, brushing by Daxton.

"And you," responded the young girl. "Did you get my obble?"

"I was just about to reply," Del said. "I didn't believe you earlier today when you said they were so large and so close."

"I told you, it's just a matter of time," the girl said, her hands moving wildly.

"So, the rumors are true about Ambassador Vulkan not being able to stabilize the islands," Del said, in a small voice. "I'm afraid of what will happen if it gets much worse."

What gets worse?

"I thought your mom wouldn't let you come back this year," Del continued, tilting her head.

"Yes, that's what I am dying to talk to you about," Electra said, lowering her voice a bit. "I couldn't send it in an obble."

"Well, I would love to hear about it, but I am kind of busy?" Del replied, canting her head over her shoulder toward Daxton, Tiffany, and Brent.

"Hello there, I am Electra Ambrose, descendant of Alaina Ambrose, founder of mine and Del's Society," Electra said, smiling.

"Hi." Brent waved, pushing his glasses back on his nose.

"Hello," Tiffany said, staring at the beautiful robe.

Daxton felt his satchel move and quickly took his hand to it, but it was too late; Brea and then Blaze ran down his leg, out from under the robe, and then flew over his head before landing on either shoulder.

"Brea! Blaze!" he called, frustrated.

The air shifted around him, and he looked to see Electra and Del staring at him.

What? Do I have egg on my face?

"Eleagons!" Electra said, her eyes opening wide with fear.

"Yeah," he said nervously.

"What are you doing with them?" Del asked.

Daxton's day was just getting better and better. If he had known what he was doing with eleagons, he could answer his own questions as to what he really was.

What does she mean? They're mine, they found me.

"I hatched them," he said. He wanted to sound confident, but knew he failed.

"Have you come to destroy what is left of Eldragor?" Electra demanded.

Daxton saw her palm flip over and he thought she was ready to attack. "No!" he stated quickly, opening his satchel for Brea and Blaze to return and hide.

"Eleagons were found to have started the Rift years ago. They are responsible for killing hundreds of people!" Electra said.

"That's just not possible," Daxton said. He knew his eleagons, and they would never do a thing like that.

"Those were dark eleagons," Del said. "They were hatched from evil."

"They were banned for what they did," Electra retorted. "And with the Eternal Tree in its state, these could wipe us out."

"They're babies!" Daxton replied. "Not evil!" Daxton argued as Brea and Blaze flew into the satchel. "They are just babies and are not evil and are not here to destroy anything or any tree!"

"They're not going to hurt the Eternal Tree?" Del asked with a raised brow.

"They would never do that." He wasn't sure what the Eternal Tree was, but he knew his eleagons.

"The Eternal Tree! That's what I needed to talk to you about!" Electra looked around like she was making sure no one else was nearby. "The Eternal Tree is dying. Ambassador Vulkan only has three amulets. He's been using an ancient method to keep the island together. If he cannot complete his method, all will be lost. There will be no more power for us to regenerate. Our world will die," Electra went on.

"That's impossible," Del said.

"I would not have believed it either. I told you, Mom didn't want me coming back this year because of the rumored sighting of a vorous beast. Well, they caught a guy trespassing and determined he was using his own shadow to hide his presence, and someone mistook that for a vorous beast. Apparently, he was looking for the missing amulet. And then the storms... ."

"Yes, the storms are getting worse." Del agreed, looking at Electra.

"It's because the tree is dying."

"What do you mean your world will die?" Daxton asked. Almost everything she said was hard for him to understand, but that word stuck out for him.

"Just that, die. And so will your eleagons."

"How?" Daxton asked, shifting his weight as his eyebrows arched. He was very worried, and it was written all over her face.

"Eleagons have to be near their source element to pull energy from. If they are not, then they will die. This is sort of their habitat. They don't have to stay here a hundred percent of the time, but they must return here every now and then," Del said like it was obvious.

"What Society are they going in? Who is their host sponsor?" Electra asked with a look of disgust. "Madame Pearl has said nothing about anyone with those things."

"Those THINGS?" Daxton yelled.

"Yes, Daxton. Eleagons are not seen as friendly here because they are responsible for the death and destruction of so much," Del said quietly. "They are like a bad omen."

"I can't even understand the words that are coming out of your mouth. How can something as tiny as a cotton ball hurt anyone?"

"Nothing ever starts out as evil; it evolves into evil," Electra stated.

"But these are just babies," Del conceded. "And they're pure."

"They could still evolve into something evil!"

"That's nonsense," Brent said. "For something to evolve into evil it must have evil or find it, and as Daxton said, that is just not possible."

"If they were banned, then Mrs. Fancy Pants would not have brought us from Georgia," Tiffany said.

"Georgia. Georgia?" Electra's eyes grew wide. "You're from the NORMAL LANDS?"

This conversation keeps getting better and better. We're definitely not blending in.

"I think that's what it's referred to by your people," Brent said matter-of-factly.

"So, you're telling me, not only did Theresa bring Normals to the Islands, but she also brought a boy that happened to hatch eleagons that could be good or evil. It's no wonder that my mother didn't want me to come this year." She took a deep breath, her brows furrowed in concentration. "And anyone could take those things and use them for who knows what."

"Well, the only way to break the bond would be for, well, you know," Del said.

"No. I don't know," Daxton said, afraid of what the answer might be.

"Death!" Electra said. "To break the bond is by death. Once that happens, the eleagons go back to elemental form."

The wind picked up and Daxton watched as the two hugged each other and Electra hurried off.

"Sorry about that," Del said.

"It's okay," Daxton said, even though none of this felt okay.

CHAPTER 8 - STUDENTS

Del looked at the three. "All right, take note, please. Many others, and I do mean many, will not care for you to be here because of where you come from, or what you brought with you. You should keep that information to yourself."

Daxton nodded.

"The other thing you need to be careful of are the instabilities leftover from the Rift."

Brent's eyes widened and he looked to Daxton.

"There is that word again, Rift," Daxton said. "What is the Rift?"

Del looked like she was gathering her thoughts; picking her words carefully, "The Rift is an evil chaos of elemental power that tears through the land," Del said, pointing to a dark tree line, then to a large crack in the ground, and finally to an overgrown area. It

THE ELEAGONS AND THE ELEMENTAL RIFT

looked like it formerly contained a building. "That section is known as the Pitch, for the high screams that were heard the night of the Rift. No one goes there now for fear of creatures that may be there."

"What types of creatures?" Daxton asked, looking around at the people coming and going. With so many dangers around, it was no wonder that this place looked empty.

"There have been reports of man-eating plants and strange creatures, but I am not so sure they are true," Del said. "The point is, it's important to remember that you are safe so long as you don't go near the Pitch."

"Doesn't this place have some sort of enchantment to protect it?" Tiffany asked, flipping her palm open trying to summon the air, but nothing happened.

Del looked at Tiffany, "Enchantment? There are a few guards, known as Mayhem Riders, who patrol the areas surrounding the grounds, but enchantments are just in your fairy tales."

"Mayhem Riders? I haven't seen anyone patrolling the grounds," responded Tiffany. "Are you sure?"

Del huffed. "Don't you understand? That's the point. They are always watching. They don't want to be seen. They have a lot to cover. If you can't see them, you don't know where they are. They could be watching us right now."

Tiffany just stared back at Del before turning away and rolling her eyes.

Daxton looked around and noticed there were a handful of students and teachers gathered in groups around four elemental flags flying on flagpoles in sections for elementors to stand. There were bubbits from all four elements serving various foods. Teachers and returning students wore robes of beautiful colors and

85

patterns, which Daxton assumed symbolized their elements. In the center of the far end of the area was a cloud that acted as a podium.

A student with long, white hair approached the group. With every confident step, her hair bounced behind her. She had a pearl headpiece with a brilliant blue stone in the center that shone brightly in the sun. Her robe was covered in seashells and bright coral. She had to be in the same society as Del. As she got closer, Daxton realized that the stone on her headpiece perfectly matched her eyes. The confidence in her stride told him that this coordination was something she planned. She was taller than Del.

"Del! There you are," the girl said. "Madame Pearl has been looking for you. The ceremony is about to begin." She looked over at Daxton and lifted her chin higher before continuing. "Electra said you were doing something for Madame Theresa. She has her own monitor, Preston, who can do her errands. You have more important things to do." She looked at the three behind Del. "Do they speak or just stand there?"

Daxton took a step forward, watching Tiffany from the corner of his eye. "Yeah, we speak," Daxton said, not liking her attitude.

"We do more than speak," Tiffany said, balling her fist.

Del smiled and answered quickly, "I will be to see Madame Pearl just as soon as I drop them off at the Aeroious tent. It's fine, Blair."

"Well, at least they won't be in our tent," Blair said, squinting at the three.

"Blair, this is Tiffany, Daxton, and Brent," Del said, motioning the three of them. "This is Blair Luxador."

"Nice to meet you," Daxton spoke, offering his hand in a gesture of goodwill.

Del stepped in front of him and shot him a warning glare.

Daxton lowered his hand. Obviously shaking hands was something they didn't do here.

I wonder if Theresa has some plan to get past the stigma of people from the Normal Lands.

"Yes," Tiffany said, catching Del's reaction to Daxton's hand.

"You as well," Brent nodded, straightening his shoulders.

"Blair!" called a tall boy wearing a dark blue robe as he quickly approached them. He was effortlessly handsome, with a string of silver pearls resting on his forehead like a crown, almost glowing against his blue-black hair. "The ceremony is starting soon, and you need to be perfect. Now come on."

"This is Xander Luxador, Blair's brother," Del said.

The boy nodded to the three and grabbed Blair's arm. "We shall not be late."

"Xander, this is Daxton, Tiffany, and Bre...," Del was cut off.

"Del, not now. I will meet them if they last," he retorted, pulling Blair with him. "If you will excuse us, we are needed elsewhere."

"Well, now you've met the Luxador siblings," Del said, rolling her eyes. "Let's get you to your places like Madame Theresa requested."

They followed Del to the outside of the purple tent that had banners with the air symbol, swirls inside a triangle.

"This is where I will leave you," Del said. "This is where all the new students they think will be in Aero go before the ceremony."

"They think?" Daxton asked.

"Yes, only the quill truly decides," Del said, leaving.

Daxton gazed at the tent with a sense of pride.

This could be where I belong.

Just when he was about to move forward, a drop of water hit his forehead. There wasn't a cloud in the sky. How weird.

The tent's canopy was big enough to hold at least fifty people under it. There were a few other kids around his age in black robes and several older kids in purple robes that had gold etching of triangles.

In the back was a table with different drinks and snacks, all purple. Purple and silver bubbits floated around the tent, offering more snacks, even to people who already had them. Some bubbits were running around and two collided into one another. Daxton laughed, watching two others fight over a tray of drinks. The darker purple one with one eye kicked the other one and jumped on top of him while holding the tray for Daxton to get a drink from.

Daxton picked up a mug that had a purple drink in it with lots of smoke coming from the top and took a big swig. He was thirstier than he thought and kept drinking. From the corner of his eye, he saw Brent take a drink as well.

Tiffany was busy looking at the bubbits while smiling and running her fingers over one of their gooey heads. When Daxton finished drinking his drink, in front of him were a pair of tall, muscular boys. The boys stared at him oddly and he offered a smile in response as butterflies crept in his stomach, making him feel nervous about what they might say or ask. Daxton didn't want any trouble; he just wanted a place to belong. He looked to Brent, who seemed to be lost in his own world, and then to Tiffany, who was busy fussing with her hair.

Tiffany must be trying to make a good impression.

"Hi, I'm Bjorn," the shorter of the two boys said, shifting his weight. He had olive skin, brown eyes, and dark hair. His robe was plain. Instead of everything that the girls from the Aquaious society had, the only adornment was a large purple brooch made of feathers.

Daxton met his eyes. "I'm Daxton." This was the best he could come up with. He was not sure how to start a conversation or what to even talk about. Everything seemed so different here. Daxton wasn't a big sports fan and the only real hobby he had was sketching. He wasn't even sure if they did that here. A moment of awkward silence went by before the other boy spoke up.

"I'm Ivan," said the taller boy, standing there exchanging looks with Bjorn. Ivan had big feet covered in huge boots and dark skin that was accented with armbands. His dark hair was long and pulled back in a simple ponytail. He had a scruffy face and pimples on his chin. The most interesting thing about him was his eyes; one pupil looked like a snake's.

"Nice to meet you," Daxton replied, nodding his head to the left as a signal for Brent and Tiffany to speak up, and then rolled his eyes when they didn't. He shrugged his shoulders, giving them an awkward look. "This is Brent and that is Tiffany."

Tiffany looked over at the sound of her name. "I'm thirsty and because no bubbits are handing me any drinks, nor is Mrs. Fancy Pants going to offer me any, I was wondering if there is a place to get something to drink or if all newcomers just die of dehydration or something so you can feed us to a beast later?" Tiffany said, offering a smile.

Why is she talking like that?

Daxton pinched the spot between his eyes in shock.

Here I am trying to make a good impression and there goes Tiffany running her mouth.

"What was all that about?" Bjorn asked once Tiffany was far enough away to not hear him.

"Long journey," Daxton answered.

"Let me point out a few other people," Bjorn said, pointing to a thin boy with a purple robe. "That is Preston. He is the society's flawless one and is Madame Theresa's favorite.

Daxton took note of Preston and his attire. He had many pairs of colorful glasses and a notebook in every pocket of his robe. His purple robe was not long, being cut a bit short above his bony ankles, and had many alchemy symbols. His bow tie was two very distinct triangles. There was not a piece out of place of his perfect, dark chocolate hair.

Bjorn pointed. "The girl beside him with flowers in her hair is Iris." He moved his finger to point at another section of students. "The three girls over there who will never shut up are Zoey, Catherine, and Jessica."

Just as Bjorn spoke, the three girls walked over, all smiling.

Daxton had not gotten his story down just right and didn't want to make a fool of himself. He knew not to offer his hand. Standing up straight, he took his hands to his robe and made sure it was nice and neat.

"Hello, you must be Bjorn Dryke," Zoey said.

Bjorn nodded. "And you're Zoey Zephyrine. I heard your name being called when we were taking the picture. The gems in your hair kept blinding me."

"Sorry about that. My mom kept adding them," Zoey replied, her cheeks turning red.

"Hello, I'm Daxton," Daxton interjected, shifting his weight

"I didn't see you at the picture ceremony," Zoey stated, tilting her head.

"Yeah, um," Daxton stumbled over his words, not knowing what ceremony she was talking about. "I might take it later," he added, giving her a fake smile.

"Okay?" Zoey stated, arching her eyebrow. "Well, let me help introduce you to a few others. This is Catherine de' Medici Drake and Jessica Onyx," Zoey said, pointing to each of the girls. Zoey was tall with shoulder-length braided hair, ivory skin, a heart-shaped face, and a few freckles on her nose. She appeared to be the leader of the trio.

Daxton nodded, but he was terrible with names. Even if he had been told about Catherine and Jessica twice, he probably wouldn't remember. The only one that he might remember would be Iris because she had purple flowers in her hair.

"Where's your purple artifact?" Zoey asked. "It's a tradition for an Aeroious elementor to take something purple to the Worthiness Ceremony."

"Must have dropped it," Daxton said, not having any idea what Zoey was talking about.

"Doesn't your family believe in tradition?" Jessica asked, squinting her hazel eyes at Daxton as if he was the plague.

"Yeah, my brooch has been in the family for years and my mother would kill me if I lost it," Catherine said, moving her hands to touch her wine-colored briolette broach. Compared to her friends, she stuck out. Her sapphire eyes were mesmerizing and her long, ashen hair shined. Daxton felt some kind of connection to her, but he didn't know why.

"I am, uh the, um," Daxton paused for a moment. "The first in my family."

Each of the girls gasped.

"That means you will be very weak," Catherine spoke quickly, avoiding eye contact.

"Nonsense," Zoey spoke. "Just because he is the first, well," she paused for a moment. "Well, just because it has happened to the others," she paused again and smiled. "You will do just fine."

Catherine grabbed Zoey's and Jessica's hands. "Come, girls, let's get to the front of the line. It was nice to meet you, Daxton."

Daxton nodded as they left and looked over at Ivan and Bjorn and asked, "Does anything purple work?"

"It's usually something your family gives you," Ivan explained, looking sheepishly at Bjorn.

"But I guess anything will work," Bjorn announced.

Daxton scrambled to find something purple because he didn't want to go out of the tent without something, but he also didn't want to use something ridiculous like a purple napkin from the snack table.

"This is for sure to get me into the Aero Society," Bjorn said in sudden excitement while pulling a purple rock out of his pocket. "Everyone in my family before me has used it and each has found their way in. It used to be bigger, but a piece was broken off each time one got accepted to the Society."

Tiffany stood in her black robe, talking to another girl who was also dressed in black. Tiffany was showing her the fork Daxton had given her the night before. Tiffany motioned Daxton over and spoke. "Daxton, this is Valerie. She is also new, and we are hoping to be roommates."

"Hello. I don't want to go to the Ignis Society. I would hate it there. It's too hot and they must sleep on lava beds. I would not mind going to the water society. I have a cousin there, but I just can't be as proper as the Luxadors in that society. I don't have much family that is Aeroious, well, maybe a great aunt or uncle, but I am not sure. I have this ribbon I am going to use for luck. What are you going to use?" She spoke very fast. Valerie was taller than Tiffany and had silver hair that was tied in a braid with a long purple ribbon that had words embroidered over. Her eyes were gray and her skin was pale. She seemed to be just as nervous as Daxton was.

Just as Daxton was about to respond, Madame Theresa appeared in the doorway in a fancy purple robe embroidered with gold triangles.

She announced, "It's time."

Daxton froze. He still didn't have anything purple on him. He thought for a moment and then looking around, an idea struck him as he saw Tiffany and Valerie move into line. Quickly, he opened his satchel and Brea's head popped out, followed by her hand grasping his fork from the other night. It had a purple stone at the end and lines of purple that made their way to the prongs. He smiled, fastening the fork to his black robe. Even though he was unsure what society he would get placed in, he had hoped that it would be Aero, and if his fork had taught him anything, it was the best was yet to come.

"Just go with the flow," Bjorn patted Daxton on his shoulder.

Daxton nodded with gratitude, making sure the pin was well attached so the fork wouldn't fall off.

When Bjorn was distracted and talking to Ivan, Daxton pulled his satchel close to his face.

"Thank you for the help," he whispered to the eleagons, "but you two need to stay hidden right now, okay? It's important."

The pair rolled their eyes but went back into the satchel. At least for now, he would blend in.

Madame Theresa walked into the tent, scanning the room until she found Brent, Tiffany, and Daxton. Quickly she pulled them aside and scanned Brent and Tiffany again and shook her head. She pulled out two small bottles filled with a purple liquid. "You need to drink this full bottle every four days. Come to me when it is empty," she said, handing the two bottles to Brent and Tiffany.

Brent and Tiffany looked at each other and took the bottles, which they each placed into a pocket..

"Very good. Don't forget, four days," reminded Madame Theresa

Theresa moved just a bit away from the three and snapped her fingers three times to get everyone's attention. "The new students will be called one by one. You will stand in the center where you see markings on the ground. Madame Margaret will announce your name, then the quill will light up different symbols on the platform around you before drawing a triangle in midair above your head with your name in it." She paused for a moment. "Preston will be taking notes, but the quill is what will officially register you in Eldragor. After your name has been registered, do not return to this tent, but wait for Preston to hand you your new robe. Is everyone clear?"

Daxton didn't feel clear about anything, but this kind of made sense. He was supposed to stand and wait for the quill to do its dance. He was nervous, but he thought he could do at least that one thing right today. He held his hand to the lump where the pendant rested underneath his robe and clothes. His hand started to burn slightly causing him to quickly look at his palm where he saw a flash of purple light for a split second. His eyes widened as he tried to control his shock. This was what Theresa's palm looked like earlier. Daxton crossed his fingers. Maybe, just maybe, this meant he was going to have an array.

Looking at the lines on his palm, questions weighed heavy on his mind.

Will I become an elementor? Could this be home for me? Will I be able to keep the eleagons?

He was out of his depth here. As his hand went to the fork pinned to his robe, his smile grew.

The best is yet to come.

CHAPTER 9 - THE WORTHINESS CEREMONY

Madame Theresa pulled back the heavy tent flaps and led the new students out. As they made their way out in a single file line, Daxton noticed a woman with long, white hair walking to the front of the stage. An elaborate white feathered cape was draped over her shoulders. Floating behind her was a small purple feather that zigzagged as she made her way to a small, raised podium. She seemed so beautiful and graceful that Daxton had no idea how old she was.

As a gust of wind ruffled the feathers of her cloak, she glanced over to the line of students walking from the purple tent and it seemed like her deep blue eyes locked onto Daxton's. With a snap of her fingers, thousands of various colored bubbles filled with confetti swirled out from behind, spreading throughout the area.

"Welcome to Eldragor and the Worthiness Ceremony for new students," she began. "I am Madame Margaret, Governess of the Wind. The Aero Society is honored to host the ceremony this year." Madame Margaret lowered her head into a kind of half-bow toward the audience. "I want to welcome Victor Von Stratus and the governors of each of the Eldragor Societies."

"This quill," Madame Margaret continued, "has been used in the Worthiness Ceremony for centuries. It has determined the acumen and skill of each of you in the audience. It's a powerful instrument and we must all trust and accept the judgment of the quill. Just remember, no matter the outcome, you are worthy of being at Eldragor."

Daxton had never seen a feather like this one before. Its barbs were red, pink, apple green, indigo, robin egg blue, and more. The colors seemed to dance on the feather as if a light were shining on it. The center of the quill looked like gold, and the tips of the barbs curled wildly in every direction. There was so much energy stored in it, and it hadn't even done anything yet. He couldn't wait to see it in action.

The quill flew up from the dais and circled the stage, as if looking at everyone in their seats. The small crowd in the stands whistled and cheered.

Daxton saw the quill dance around Madame Margaret, brush against her cheek for a moment, and then bob next to her.

"Let us begin," she said looking over to the fire section. "Our first inductees will be the children of the Ignis Society. Headmaster Eldrige," Madame Margaret announced.

Daxton saw a stocky man dressed in an elaborate red robe embroidered with gold flames march down the aisle, followed by a dozen or more children in black robes. They stopped at the edge of the red carpet, each student waiting to walk up the stone steps to the stage.

The first to walk up was a set of twin boys that had red, spiky hair. The quill turned fiery red and spun with a crackle of fire as it moved to hover over the boys for a moment before moving to the fire alchemy symbols in the stones where it began to etch. The quill moved back and forth between the boys and the stones.

Daxton stood on his tiptoes with his eyes glued to the quill.

It looks like it is going to poke their eyes out.

The students rubbed their hands on the side of their pants, causing what looked like flames to burn and sizzle. Soon the smell of smoke filled the air. Everyone was silent as the boys' eyes followed the quill as it hovered patiently in front of them. They held out their palms and their arrays illuminated, spinning with crackling fire as the quill took its last dance around them writing their names in the fire symbol above their heads.

Daxton heard a voice echo around the courtyard. "Rory Rowan. New. Fire acumen four, but not much control." After a pause it continued, "Ronnie Rowan. New. Fire acumen three, but total control." The two boys looked at each other with grins and embraced as they turned and left the stage. The quill continued to test the fire section until all the students had their results.

Madame Margaret stepped up to the podium once again. She and Master Eldridge exchanged nods and smiles. Master Eldrige beamed as he walked off, while Madame Margaret turned her attention to the green section with a kind smile not leaving her face. "Madame Gia Bionity of the Terrina Society," she announced.

A chubby woman with what looked like orange paint-dipped hair walked over to the stage, followed by children all dressed in black. Daxton liked that Madame Gia Bionity had lots of little colorful animals around her, including at least one that Daxton had never seen before. It was a small furry creature with bright pink fur. It looked almost like a mix between a rabbit and a cat. Her robe was made of green leaves and ended in a long train that reached almost all the way back to the green tent as she walked toward the stage. There were as many girls as boys, and each seemed to wear either a seed or a branch for their good luck totem.

Daxton watched the first girl take the steps to the stage, and the now green quill took flight, halting over the girl in the center. This girl had to be older; there was no way she was twelve. She had a quiver and bow over her shoulder and brown leather laced boots. He could see her red fire hair braided down her back. Daxton had not seen anyone else with a bow and watched as she stepped very carefully and listened.

The quill danced around her, drawing shapes of triangles and circles. When it flew back to the center podium, Daxton heard the familiar voice call out, "Athena Hunter. New. Terrina acumen five with medium control."

The ceremony continued as each of the new initiates took the stage and then the quill giving their results.

Finally, it came down to the last girl in the society. Daxton observed her carefully because she looked just as nervous as he felt. The quill did its dance and wrote her name above her head in green and orange. When the quill returned to the podium, Madame Margaret's voice boomed across the stadium. "Eve Cain. New. Terrina. Acumen level one. Control medium." Eve looked over at Daxton and gave him a smile. Daxton smiled back, watching her go back to her section and get dressed in a new green robe.

Daxton hoped the Aero Society would be next, but Madame Margaret turned to the opposite side of him and began to introduce the Aquaious Society, led by Madame Pearl, a tall woman dressed in a light blue gown decorated with an intricate pattern of pearls.

Daxton felt his satchel pump him in the side and knew Brea and Blaze were getting restless. He looked down and whispered, "Do you want to get stolen? Just hang on. It can't last forever."

Blair took the stage wearing a black robe. The quill danced and twilled around her until the voice rang out again. "Blair Luxador. New. Aqua. Acumen level four with medium control."

Daxton heard whispers and cheers from the small crowd. Blair walked down the stage to where her brother waited, beaming, and immediately took off her black robe as many bubbits came to help put on her blue robe. She waved to the crowd.

Eventually, all of the Aquaious students were registered, and Daxton knew it was time for Aero. Both nerves and excitement filled his chest. This was it.

"Madame Theresa Thornton of the Aero Society," Madame Margaret's voice rang out over the stadium. Madame Theresa stiffened her stance and one by one each of the children followed in line behind her.

"Valerie Von Stratus," Madame Theresa called. Daxton caught a hint of stress in her voice, but it was like she was trying to hide it.

Valerie climbed the stone steps to the stage. The quill took off and danced around her as she looked like she was going to vomit. After what seemed forever, the feather turned purple and shot out a thick silver ink making lines all over her silhouette before stopping above her head and then drawing a triangle. Valerie's eyes lit up as she realized she was officially in the Aero Society. "Valerie Von Stratus. New. Air acumen level three with medium control."

Next in line was Catherine. The quill lifted from the center, shaking and turning as it danced around her body before stopping at her head. With a zigzag, it drew a triangle above her head that changed from dark blue to purple. "Catherine de' Medici Drake. New. Air acumen level four with medium control."

One by one, each of the other students was examined by the quill. For Bjorn, it drew more than one triangle, and for Ivan, it drew a triangle all around his body. For Halo Hallon, a girl he had seen in the tent, the quill drew a small purple triangle with two green ones on each of its sides. Zoey's was three small purple triangles. Each smiled at their results.

"Bjorn Dryke. New. Air acumen level three with low control."

"Ivan Brook. New. Air acumen one with low control."

"Zoey Zephyrine. New. Air acumen level two with medium control."

Right before Daxton was Iris Crenshaw, who fixed her flower in her hair before carefully taking the stone steps to the stage. The quill did just as before but drew four dark purple triangles. One above her head with swirly curls in it, another at her feet, and one on each of her palms. Her acumen was level one with low control.

Finally, it was his turn. He took a deep breath, trying to prepare himself.

It's not a big deal. Everyone else did it. You can do it too.

"Daxton," Madame Margaret called out.

Daxton? Why aren't they saying my last name?

Daxton felt Theresa nudge him forward as butterflies grew in his stomach. He took each rocky step up with his eyes set on the quill, which danced with joy awaiting its next applicant. Finally, he came to stand in the center of four interlocking triangles. The one in the northern spot was pointed up and had a horizontal line through it. The southern one was similar but pointing down instead. The east and west triangles didn't have lines, and one was pointed up and the other down. The symbol of Eldragor.

Daxton felt the weight of the air was no longer weightless, but as though one hundred pounds had been stacked onto his shoulders. His mouth grew dry, and his vision blurred. He slowly stretched his hand out and the quill took off dancing around him again, lighting up the engraved alchemy symbols inside the Eldragor symbol and changing colors. The quill started drawing colorful triangles all around him. It began to write a letter T in the corner of the triangle above his head. Almost immediately the quill exploded with color, turning black, stopping, and falling over lifeless.

Daxton could feel every pair of eyes on him. He wanted the ground to open up and swallow him. Suddenly, he felt a hand on his shoulder.

"Smile and wave," a man's voice said.

Daxton didn't move as he watched the man flick his wrist to levitate the lifeless quill.

"Ceremony over!" Madame Margaret said as confetti burst from the stage.

"What happened?" Daxton asked, his fingers trembling, voice shaking.

"Come now," the man's voice said. "The quill has finished."

Daxton looked up to see a tall blond man with dark eyes

encircled by a wispy white smoke crackling with unknown energy. His dark red robe could barely be seen, hidden under an even darker red cloak. His lips were a straight line as he glanced at Daxton. Everything about him said he was confident and not to be trifled with.

"Ambassador Devon Vulkan," Madame Theresa said as she quickly walked up to Daxton. "It is good to see you."

"And you, Theresa," Vulkan said, his hand still on Daxton. "You must be very proud this young man got registered in the Aero Society."

Is that what just happened?

"Careful with that bag there," Ambassador Vulkan said, turning to leave.

Careful with my bag? How did he see my bag? Did he sense the eleagons?

CHAPTER 10 - SETTLING IN

With the ceremony over, Daxton followed Theresa back to the Aero tent, while Brent and Tiffany trailed behind.

The last thing I wanted to do was break something. How could that even happen? That man that spoke seemed okay with whatever had happened, and well, the entire stage didn't catch on fire. It could have gone worse.

The area was closing down as bubbits moved around cleaning up. Daxton watched as others returned to the castle.

"Stop messing with my stuff," Daxton heard coming from a girl who appeared to just be arriving. She was fighting to get through a cluster of wine-colored bubbits.

Her long, rainbow-colored hair was pulled back from her ivory face and violent eyes. She was taller than Daxton, but he didn't know if it was because of her high black leather boots or not. A cool breeze quickly arose. A storm was coming.

"Raizy," Madame Theresa scolded.

"They started it," Raizy insisted, as the bubbits ran off.

"Raizy, control yourself before we are all blown away by your storm," commanded Madame Theresa, her mouth becoming a line.

"Just let me zap one!" Raizy said, her voice rising.

"No!" Madame Theresa replied.

"What are you looking at?" Raizy asked, her eyes darting to Daxton and then to h's satchel. "What's wrong with your bag?"

"Nothing," Daxton said quickly, realizing he had the bag on the outside of his purple robe. He couldn't let them out, not with what he'd heard about eleagons, but Brea and Blaze seemed to have their own opinions on when to be seen. This was going to be a long eight weeks, he realized.

"Zeke," Madame Theresa said, looking over Daxton's shoulder, "Preston is busy, so please show our new students to their rooms."

"Of course," Zeke said, turning around.

Daxton looked to see a boy about his age with dark, curly hair, and wearing a purple robe full of alchemy symbols. Daxton nodded and held his satchel close till he felt it move against his hip.

"What's with your bag?" Zeke asked, looking at Daxton's satchel.

Oh, please settle down!

Daxton's eleagons didn't settle down while entering Eldragor either. He wasn't surprised, but he hoped they would relax a little.

He already had multiple students noticing movements in the satchel, which didn't seem good. As they moved through the great chamber, Daxton admired a large painting, under which read,

Ambassador Gabriel Luxador, founder of the Eternal Tree.

Around the painting were four other, smaller portraits. They all looked similar to the giant one in front of him. Each had a name under it.

Dagon, Douglas, Blake, and Markus Luxador. I wonder what they all did to get portraits here.

"I see you are studying my great ancestors. That pleases me and my family greatly, but there is no need to bow to me yet," Xander sneered from behind Daxton. Blair laughed next to him..

Daxton turned and stared at them, seething, but didn't say anything.

"Carry on," stated Xander as he and Blair continued across the hall.

As his angry and embarrassed gaze followed the movement of the two, another portrait caught Daxton's eye. It was of one of the women at the ceremony. She had a green dress and was holding a small seed in the shape of an 'S.' A smile was plastered on her face. Daxton read the caption underneath.

Madame Gia, creator of the Infinity Seed.

Daxton followed Zeke up the cloud stairs until they arrived at a wall of white, fluffy clouds that shifted and swirled before his eyes.

Cloud stairs? Cloud walls? This place is amazing.

"What's that?" Brent asked.

"An elemental barrier. It keeps out anyone who doesn't belong in the Aero Society," Zeke said proudly.

Daxton heard Zeke and became nervous. He saw Tiffany and Brent both look at their palms where Theresa had put the Aeroious symbol. He watched Zeke put his hand to the clouds and push against it. The clouds gave way and Zeke was gone.

"This thing better not mess up my hair," Tiffany said, pushing her way through.

"I guess I will see you on the other side," Brent proclaimed and followed suit.

"Yeah," Daxton replied, his heart in this throat. It looked so easy; just walk through it, but nothing ever came that easy for him and he was just waiting for the ground to open up and swallow him whole. Brent and Tiffany were lucky. Theresa made sure they would get through. He didn't have that same luxury.

With a deep breath, he walked forward, not surprised when he bounced off the wall. He bowed his head in defeat, exhaling slowly. *Now what?* It was just a confirmation that he didn't belong here. With his head on the cloud, he slowly began tapping it in defeat. Getting mad and on the verge of walking away, he felt Brea move up his arm to his head. With her little snout, she pushed on the cloud. The cloud dissolved under his head and Daxton fell forward to the other side.

"Welcome home!" Tiffany said.

Home!

The feeling of belonging registered in his mind as he looked around. Little bubbles floated around the room, carrying books, paper, or quills. The furniture in the Aero chamber was decorated in many different shades of purple with silver highlights. A huge fireplace was nestled in the back. To the left was a beverage station that was so big it looked like it belonged in a coffee house; it was filled with grinders, beakers, and anything you could think of to add flavor to your drink. Hot cocoa, coffee, and tea surrounded the space.

At least I'll never go thirsty.

"Daxton, you and Brent will be sharing a room. Tiffany, you will be sharing a room with Raizy," Zeke said,

"Raizy, that girl with colored hair?" Tiffany asked, sipping hot cocoa.

"Yep, that's her," Zeke replied. "She's, um, she's kind of stormy if you know what I mean. But she's not a monsoon or a cyclone or anything."

"What room are Daxton and I in?" Brent asked, yawning.

"201. It's the last one on the right," Zeke replied, "Madame Theresa wanted you to watch this before you went to bed," he said, illuminating his purple array.

Zeke hovered his array over four triangles, each representing an element. The triangles spun and opened until many life-like images filled the room.

Daxton felt he had stepped into an otherworldly zoo. There were frogs that burped wads of dirt, birds made of fire, transparent monkeys, water serpents, wolves with grass for fur, and countless others.

An array can do all of this? Are we going to learn to do this too?

A deep male voice rang out as the images began to move. "Long ago, elemental creatures appeared across the world. They were seen as dangerous creatures that were hunted and killed by non-elementals known as Negments. A secret society of elementors, known as Eldragor was formed to assist in teaching those with powers, as well as to provide a place to study elemental creatures. Ambassador Gabriel Luxador, an explorer, botanist, and powerful elementor, discovered a path to each of the elemental planes. The planes were dangerous, but Gabriel found a way to harness each elemental plane to create the Eternal Tree. The Eternal Tree grew into four islands. It is the center that holds our world together. We owe him our gratitude for creating a stable and peaceful place to live."

History lesson. Okay, cool.

Soon, the images disappeared. Daxton had seen many creatures, but none that looked like Brea or Blaze.

Maybe they don't want us to know because of what that girl said. But they're not evil. I know they're not.

He felt his satchel bump him again.

"Why is your bag moving again?" Zeke asked. "That bag is incredible. Your family must be very fortunate to have something like that."

Now is as good a time as any.

Daxton opened his satchel. Brea leapt out and stretched her misty wings, soaring up and turning flips in midair.

"An eleagon!" Zeke said in surprise. His eyes grew fearful. "No one has seen one for years. How did you tame one?"

"This is Brea and Blaze," Daxton said as Blaze popped his head out of the bag. "I hatched them."

"Two?! Are they, uh, are they okay?"

"Do you mean, are they dangerous?" Daxton asked, remembering what he'd heard earlier. "No, they're good. They wouldn't hurt anybody."

Zeke relaxed at the words. "What family heritage are you from again?"

Daxton hadn't thought about this. They didn't use his name at the ceremony, so was he supposed to now? It didn't seem like the best idea, especially not with how Zeke just reacted to Brea and Blaze. Daxton knew that they were not to tell anyone about the way Madame Theresa's healing brewtion didn't work on them, or that she had imprinted on Tiffany and Brent to get them in. It seemed like the people in Eldragor weren't all trustworthy. However, Zeke seemed okay, but who knew if that was true, and who knew who might overhear them?

"I am, um, a Jenkins?" He wasn't sure if that was good enough, but at least he answered. He would need to remember that name if it came up again. He couldn't go around giving everyone a different last name.

"I don't know them. Wait! You hatched them?"

"Yes."

"You didn't find them?"

"No, I hatched them," Daxton said, growing annoyed.

"They weren't already formed when you found them?"

Am I speaking in riddles?

"Long story short, I found eggs and they hatched," Daxton nervously explained.

"That's interesting." Zeke leaned forward, inspecting Brea.

"Why?"

"Eleagons aren't hatched, they are found."

"How do you know?"

"I am an Aires," Zeke said, like Daxton should know exactly what that meant.

"And?"

"Aaron Aires founded the Aero Society. He studied the elemental creatures and the eleagons."

"Oh, yeah him." Daxton had no clue who he was talking about.

"You really should keep them out of sight," Zeke whispered. "They are banned here."

"Why?"

"Some people blamed them for the Rift because they are so powerful."

"How can they be blamed for the Rift?"

"Many years ago, there was a very weak family that used them to make themselves stronger in air. That caused the Rift and all of these terrible storms. They sometimes call it the Veil of Darkness because of how terrible it's been for everyone here since her death."

"Her death?" Daxton questioned.

"Yeah, Ambassador Annya Luxador was killed the night the Rift broke out."

"How?"

"Some say it was murder by her own hand."

"How can you murder yourself?" Tiffany asked.

"Can't really," Zeke said.

"What do you think happened?" asked Daxton.

"Lord Dominus murdered her," Zeke said, nodding. "He had help, that's for sure," he added, looking down at Blaze.

"That's horrible," Daxton said, also looking down at Blaze. He pet Blaze's head, knowing his eleagons would never do something like that.

"It was then they were banned because one can use them to control elements they don't have."

"Who is Lord Dominus?" Tiffany asked

"Well," Zeke said, "I don't really know who he is. He might not even be a he."

"So, no one knows?" inquired Tiffany.

"Nope," Zeke said with a shrug. It seemed like he didn't want to talk about it anymore.

"That thing you said earlier, why can't people have two or more elements?" Brent asked.

"You three sure ask a lot of questions. Using your primary element takes a lot of energy; using a secondary element takes even more; and using a third can push you into unconsciousness or death if you're not strong enough," Zeke said.

"What happens when you use all your energy?" Brent asked.

"You have to regenerate it by resting near your element. For example, an Aquaious elementor rests near water or near an elemental creature of water."

"Elemental creatures? You mean like the ones we saw, like eleagons?" Brent asked, watching Brea and Blaze.

"Yes, like eleagons, but it was only a few that were ever actually able to train one, to have one sit there like that." Zeke turned to Daxton. "Are you sure you're from the Jenkins family?"

"As far as I know."

Daxton wasn't lying; he truly didn't know.

"Jenkins could be an old elemental family line that is less powerful." Zeke said.

"What does that mean?" Daxton asked, petting Brea.

"What's important is that you passed through the barrier," replied Zeke, obviously not wanting to go more into it.

"So, no elementor can control all four elements?" Brent asked.

"Correct. Technically it's impossible," Zeke said. "Even if you found an eleagon or something that would allow you to use the element opposite your primary one, the consequences could be dangerous."

"How dangerous? Is this the danger Madame Theresa was talking about?" Daxton asked.

"No," Zeke paused, "the danger is the Eternal Tree."

"What do you mean?" Daxton asked.

"Rumor has it that the Eternal Tree is dying. Eldragor will be ruined if we can't figure out what to do. Ambassador Vulkan is performing more experiments, but nothing seems to be working."

Lightning flashed so bright it felt like Daxton was staring at it, but he wasn't even near a window. Quickly, thunder rolled loudly outside, shaking the room they were in.

Zeke merely sighed at this.

"Why don't they just grow another tree?" Tiffany asked.

"You can't just grow a new tree. You need the four elemental stones or four things from the planes," Zeke said.

"Why not go get them?" Tiffany asked.

"The paths to the elemental planes are gone."

"Then why don't the elementors move?" Tiffany asked, tilting her head.

"There were too many accidents with elementors being away from a pure source of energy for too long," Zeke said, looking around. "There's something else I have to tell you. Some students lost their elemental powers completely and were sent away from Eldragor. I had a cousin that couldn't raise his acumen when he was here and couldn't come back. When he went home, it was like he lost everything."

The silver grandfather clock rang out, startling Daxton. He was tired, but there was still so much he wanted to know. The fire turned on in the back, letting a soft glow envelop the room. Zeke had given him tons of information, but Daxton focussed on the last thing he said.

Lost everything. If I don't advance, could I lose Brea and Blaze and never come back?

Rattled, Daxton continued in thought. I can't lose this place. Not now. Not ever.

"I didn't realize how late it was. Big day tomorrow with classes starting." Zeke said before making his way down the hall to his room.

Daxton yawned. Despite the thoughts coursing through his head, it had been a long day and he couldn't fight how tired he was.

"Daxton, do you think I could find something like your eleagons?" Tiffany asked while looking at Blaze.

"Why? I mean, it's possible, I guess," replied Daxton.

"Why should you be the only one with creatures like them? I could be the first Negment with an eleagon."

"You don't have an array, though."

"You didn't either, until you hatched Brea. Why wouldn't it work for me? Brent and I could both get our arrays, and we could all belong here."

"Yeah, Tiffany, we could find one," Brent said, making his way to the hallway.

"You know I could! I could start tomorrow and tomorrow comes early," Tiffany said, beaming.

"We're here, so we might as well make the most of it," Brent said.

"You're right. Night, Daxton. Night, Brent."

"Night," Daxton said, following Brent to his room. As his hand brushed the wall, a voice entered his head.

You don't belong here! Get out while you still can!

Daxton pulled his hand away like the wall was on fire.

"Are you okay?" Brent asked, glancing behind him.

What was that? There's been too much excitement today. I just need some sleep.

"Yeah," Daxton said, not wanting to say more.

The doors were all made of thick clouds, each with a number on it. Walking to the very end, Daxton found number 201. He put his hand on the clouds and the clouds disappeared, allowing the two to enter.

The room wasn't very big, but at least they didn't have to share it with more roommates. It was perfect for the two of them. Floating above the floor were two beds made of clouds. The frame, the blanket, the mattress, and pillows were soft-looking clouds. Between the beds was a cloud-shaped desk with a lamp that puffed smoke. It was like walking into a dream.

"This is awesome," Brent said, getting into the cloud bed. "I'll never have to make my bed again."

Daxton took Brea and Blaze out of his satchel and placed them on the cloud bed where they curled into one another as they fell to sleep.

"Goodnight, Brent," Daxton said, getting into his cloud bed. Soft, warm clouds snuggled around him. His day had been filled with excitement and mystery. He grabbed the pendant, hoping for a flash of purple light from his array, but it didn't appear. Sighing, he rolled over, his excitement from just minutes ago gone.

How weak am I?

CHAPTER 11 - DAY ONE

Daxton awoke, excited to take on the day. This place still confused him, but he wouldn't let that stop him from finding out everything he could. He was ready for Eldragor.

Making his way downstairs and then outside to look for Brent and Tiffany, he saw that girl with the rainbow hair standing by a tree. Looking around, he saw a lot of students from the ceremony yesterday, but not his two friends.

Where are those two?

Daxton continued to look around and saw Tiffany's roommate. "Hey, Raizy is it?" he asked as he got her attention.

"Who's asking?

"Me, Daxton."

"Oh, you're that boy I saw yesterday with the new girl. Tonya, no Tina."

"Tiffany? Your roommate?."

"Yeah, her."

"Have you seen her?" Daxton asked.

"She went with some boy that had glasses to go get their schedules," Raizy answered.

"That's Brent," Daxton said.

"Don't care, you three won't be here long enough for me to remember," Raizy said, fixing her rainbow ponytail.

What?

"What's that supposed to mean?"

"Nothing."

"Is that why they call you 'stormy?'"

"Who called me stormy?"

"I don't know," Daxton said, feeling his satchel bump against him.

"What's up with your bag?" Raizy asked, looking at him.

Not this again.

"Nothing," Daxton said, hoping Brea and Blaze would just settle down.

Raizy flipped the flap open on the satchel and Brea and Blaze quickly popped their heads out, happy at the prospect of being released.

"Baby eleagons!" Raizy beamed.

Daxton moved his hand to Brea and Blaze, looking at Raizy as if she had punched him in his face. He jabbed their tiny heads down and then flipped the satchel's flap closed. "Look," he murmured, looking into Raizy's eyes, filled with anger. "Where I come from, we don't just go around touching other people's stuff." He tugged tightly on the strap of his satchel, bringing it close to his chest. "I would appreciate it if you don't touch mine," he said as a beam of purple light glowed from his palm. He stared at his palm in surprise.

"Who are you?" Raizy asked.

Daxton could feel his body growing hot with anger as he curled his fist into a ball. Looking down, he realized that his hands were red and appeared to be on the verge of igniting.

Raizy instantly realized what was happening and spoke quickly. "Daxton, I am sorry. Please just breathe. I won't touch your stuff again. It was wrong of me."

Daxton took several deep breaths and tried not to think about what Raizy had done, only about what she said in her apology. When at last he felt that he was not going to combust, he opened his mouth and spoke, "Okay. Thank you for apologizing and for helping me calm down. I have no idea what just happened."

"Daxton, you just got so mad so quickly and then you almost... ," Raizy stopped and chose her next words carefully. "Well, I don't know what you were about to do, but I just knew I crossed a line. Don't take this the wrong way, but you have to learn to control your emotions. Our emotions tie directly to our powers. All elementors have power. Many have lots of power, but controlling that power is difficult. I have trouble controlling my powers more than most, mostly because I have only recently tried to control my emotions, so I understand. Remember, if you cannot control your anger, you could become dangerous."

Daxton wasn't sure how to respond. Luckily he didn't have to.

An obble popped overhead releasing a schedule that floated quickly into Daxton's hand. Daxton looked at it, thankful to have a distraction from Raizy, who moved away as she saw children approaching.

"Daxton, there you are!" Tiffany called as she and Brent jogged over. "We just got our schedules and wanted to read them together to see if we're in the same classes."

Daxton smiled and nodded.

"Why do some of my classes say level zero," Tiffany asked, pointing at her schedule.

"Because, you know," Brent said, pushing his glasses back to read his classes. "How could they put us in stronger classes if we didn't even get tested."

"Are you in the zero class too?" Tiffany asked, looking at him.

"I don't know," Daxton answered, not looking up.

"Wait, we only have one class a day?" Tiffany asked. "Is that going to make everything easier or harder?"

"Only one way to find out. If we're in the same classes as you, Daxton, we will see you there," Brent said, rolling his scroll up.

Daxton read his schedule:

Madame Freea Flintridge Level 1-4 Aerotion - Monday

Master Horace Hopkins Level 1-4 Horology -Tuesday

Madame Theresa Thorten Level 1-4 Array Practice - Wednesday

Master Morpheus Valdor Level 1-4 Darkness- Thursday

Madame Gia Bionity Level 1-4 Brewtion - Friday

Daxton frowned; he had no idea what any of it meant. As questions piled up in his head, a class caught his attention. He looked for Raizy, but she was already leading the new Aero students to their classes. The only other person he felt comfortable asking was Theresa.

The gongs rang out, signaling class was about to begin. Daxton saw Madam Theresa.

Now is a good time as ever.

"Madame Theresa, what is the class called Darkness? A class on shadows?" Daxton asked as he approached her.

"It's something you don't need to know. That class should not be taught here. The nerve of that man," Madame Theresa fumed, snatching the schedule from him. "How can he just decide that everyone should take Darkness? The weaker ones could get hurt."

Like me?

"When you go into that class, say very little," Madame Theresa said, handing him his schedule back. "I will see you later."

After she left, he glanced down at his schedule again.

She thinks I'm too weak.

The gongs rang out loudly again when Daxton arrived for his first class, aerotion. Brent and Tiffany were in a basic element class. He knew he belonged there too because he didn't know anything about this place or how to activate his array.

After checking the room number, Daxton cautiously opened the door to find children he recognized from the Worthiness Ceremony sitting on an assortment of clouds. On shelves were jars labeled with types of winds, such as hurricanes, tornadoes, and sandstorms, as well as categories of rain such as sleet, ice, snow, sun, shower, and fog. The room was large and open with clouds for the ceiling. Daxton didn't know if there was a roof or not because all he could see were clouds.

Daxton stood still as all eyes went to him; he felt like a fish out of water. He swallowed hard and slowly moved between the others. His ears began to burn, and he felt as though everyone was watching him and talking about him. He casually moved his left hand to his ear, hoping to cool it off. The noise around him became so loud he could hear what the girls in the front were saying.

"Daxton seems to not belong here," he heard. Looking around he could not tell who said it, and then he saw the teacher, a tall, slender woman with a long face and even longer arms walk in. Her frizzy white hair spun in every direction. She wore a loose purple jumpsuit with a long purple cloak and didn't look like any of the other teachers Daxton had seen.

"Welcome," the teacher said, flinging her cloak backward and illuminating a silver array with rings and swirls in it. One of the swirls released from her finger and flew toward the sky, which turned dark and rumbled. Clouds lowered and settled on the floor, and scrolls and quills flew across the room, hovering in front of each student. The teacher turned and said, "I am Madame

Flintridge, your teacher for aerotion, the process of manipulating air."

The clouds shifted into desks and chairs. One by one, each of the children took a seat. Daxton walked to the desk closest to him and sat.

"Air is all around us," Madame Flintridge began, holding a large purple quill as she smiled and moved over to where Daxton was sitting. "The air carries vibrations, which is how we hear. The most skilled can hear things the rest of us cannot because they are able to increase the vibrations by controlling the air. For them, this is how they turn up the volume on an otherwise unhearable sound or conversation."

"Do what?" Halo asked.

"Raise the volume. It's a technique called aerial sound, which some can use to hear what others are saying," Madame Flintridge said.

Daxton thought of his experience a few minutes ago and understood.

I have the ability to hear from far away. Now to figure out how to use it.

Madame Flintridge continued, and Daxton decided he should be taking notes. Picking up the quill that was on his desk, he realized this was something else he didn't know how to use; he had never written with a quill.

Don't they have pencils here? Or pens?

Everyone was busy writing and Daxton was just confused.

Iris, who was watching him, demonstrated how to use the quill by dipping it in a cloud then writing on the scroll. The words appeared in black.

Daxton studied her actions a few times and then did what she did. Madame Flintridge spoke for a while before she stood and pointed at the cloud desks.

"Now you will move your cloud desk with your array," Madame Flintridge said.

Daxton could feel the butterflies in his stomach, once again feeling he didn't belong. Seeing most of the other students quickly illuminate their array, it just seemed like second nature to everyone else. To Daxton, it was some foreign tool that he had no idea how to use.

Daxton opened and closed his hand several times and still nothing happened. Growing discouraged, he closed and opened his eyes and nearly freaked out when he saw Brea sitting on the edge of the cloud desk.

Can anyone see her? Surely if anyone saw her, they would say something.

Brea moved to Daxton's palm and sniffed around and pawed at his skin, probably trying to help him the only way she knew how. Brea lassoed her tail around his finger, making a ring. He smiled seeing the dainty ring and hoped it would help, but nothing happened. Brea gave up and curled in the center of his palm. His heart raced as he slightly squeezed Brea to hide her. As his fingers relaxed, he felt his hand go heavy and a light sensation moved through him. He opened his eyes to find a beautiful purple circle moving across his palm with a triangle in the center and a tiny white cloud hovering above. Brea dissolved into thin air and moved back to the satchel.

"Very good, Daxton," Madame Flintridge said. "Now more. Control the air and push it to the east. Use your forefinger and thumb, tilting your wrist to the east."

Daxton did just this. His eyes shone as his fingers trembled a bit, seeing the purple hues spin over his palm. He slowly twirled his fingers around, closing his eyes. Concentrating hard to create a breeze, he hoped it would gently turn his cloud to the east. Instead, a wild wind blew his cloud and several others into the classroom walls. Embarrassed, he apologized and tried again.

Zoey flipped her palm over and watched her array spin. Her breeze growing, she lost control and her cloud bumped into Ivan, and then flew up high above. "Stupid thing," she mumbled.

"How are you going to get it down?" Halo asked, positioning her cloud away from Zoey and Ivan.

"I don't know. A broom maybe?" Ivan said, shrugging.

"Yeah, you're smart," Zoey laughed.

Daxton laughed while watching the clouds in the room. Proud of himself, he looked to Iris, who was making her clouds into flowers.

"That's neat," Daxton said, watching them grow.

"Thanks," Iris yawned softly. "I'm so tired. I just can't sleep at night. The nurse spixie gave me lavender to help me relax. It seems to help, but I still don't get enough rest. There are too many bad feelings here."

Daxton was curious and pressed the issue. "Why?"

"Daxton, my family died here during the Rift," Iris replied sadly and bluntly.

Well, that was unexpected.

Daxton didn't know what to say and he bit his lip hoping he could change the subject. "I'm sorry, I didn't know," he said.

"I was young. I don't remember anything, but I got this the night of The Rift," Iris said in a low voice, turning her palm over.

"It looks painful," Daxton said, studying the patterns of burns on her ivory skin.

"Acid rain fell from the sky that night. My entire house disappeared. Just disintegrated. My aunt was lucky enough to escape with me on her hip," Iris shivered. "There was no place to hide except the Normal Lands."

Oh! This is new. I thought I was the only one from there.

"We have something in common then."

"It's not something I brag about. My great aunt Jasmine was sure that if I wasn't near my prime element I wouldn't bloom, but at around age five I was floating around the house, and she knew we would have to return to Eldragor. We got a little cottage on the outskirts of the Aer and lived there until I was of age to register for Eldragor.

"That's great that you got to come back," Daxton admitted.

"I guess. Aunt Jasmine would often make different brewtions for me to take so that my power would be less than what it was, so I wouldn't be that strong in the air."

This statement stunned Daxton, "You actually wanted to be weaker? Why?"

"Daxton, sometimes it is best to not draw attention."

"So, I guess it is unusual to fly at such an early age?"

"Oh yes!" Iris said.

"Did the brewtions work?" Daxton asked.

"I don't think so," Iris admitted. "I mean the only thing is I have been struggling to keep my array projected for long periods of time and the nightmares are getting worse."

"Nightmares?" Daxton asked in concern. He thought for a moment and could not remember the last time he truly had one.

"Yes, nightmares. Well, I guess they are not really nightmares, more like blackouts. It's like I am talking to you now, and then I blackout and don't remember anything. The day is gone and it's night. The healers don't know what's wrong."

"That sounds awful," Daxton said, casting his eyes low.

"It is," Iris said, fixing the flowers in her hair. "I now sleep in the nursery."

Out of the corner of his eye, Daxton saw Madame Flintridge spinning her purple array so quickly it looked almost silver.

"To split a cloud," she said loudly, joining her palms together while her cloud shifted with her. "You want to move your array, pulling to you the part of the cloud you want and leaving the other behind. Now you try."

He watched Iris take her hands together and move them about like there was glue stuck to her fingers. She did this a few times until her array illuminated and spun sideways. She let it do this until she flipped her palm over and there a little cloud formed in the center. Iris' face lit up as there in the center of her palm was a perfectly fluffy cloud.

Wow, Daxton thought, taking a deep breath. He wasn't sure he could create a cloud like Iris, but surely he could split one like

Madame Flintridge instructed. He took his hands together and he did just as Madame Flintridge had done. Nothing. His shoulders slumped and he felt his cheeks getting red. This is supposed to be simple!

He moved his fingers together, laced them, and flipped his wrist to get his array to appear. Nothing. He rolled his eyes in the back of his head and was beyond mad this time. He felt his pendant heavy on his chest and took a deep breath, squeezed his hands together, and felt them go hot, before slowly pulling them apart. A flash of black dark purple and green sparks flew from his hands. Daxton wanted to shut his hand, but he also wanted his array to appear. His eyes closed, scared to know what might happen next. He pulled his hands apart and there he could feel the warmth of the purple circles taking on shape and rotating as he thought hard about splitting the cloud. Smoke came from the center of the cloud. His heart raced, a bead of sweat ran down the side of his face. He opened his eyes to see his cloud rip in half with a thunderous roar.

"I did it. I really did it!" he nearly yelled. This was just what he needed to know that he did belong, and he was on his way to becoming an Elementor.

He didn't notice the students staring at him, wide-eyed.

"Very good, Daxton," Madame Flintridge said, walking around the room with her large fluffy cloud following behind.

Even though she praised him, she looked at him with concern in her eyes. A lot of the adults here had.

Is it because I'm new?

Daxton beamed with pride, watching his two clouds.

"Don't let your power get away from you," Bjorn whispered to Daxton.

"I won't," Daxton answered with new confidence.

"Catherine, I need you to work with Daxton on control," Madame Flintridge said. "I don't need him setting whirlwinds loose or causing massive storms, seeing that he has not had the proper entry-level education."

Daxton looked up hearing his name as the children around him began to whisper.

Entry-level education.

"Bjorn, I don't have all day to see if you can do this," Madame Flintridge said, stopping by his cloud desk, ignoring the whispers of the other children.

"I can do this in my sleep," Bjorn yawned.

"You can make all you want in your sleep," Madame Flintridge responded. "However, this is class and I need you to split your cloud."

Bjorn grinned and illuminated his silver array. He didn't have to move his hand much and his cloud split perfectly into two identical clouds.

Daxton was impressed; the two perfect clouds Bjorn split now flew smoothly around the room. He cast his eyes back toward his own little lifeless cloud that looked like poop; white fluffy poop.

"Very good," Madame Flintridge said before shooing a bird cloud away. "Amon! If your bird doesn't leave me alone I will…," she paused and glared at him, taking the annoying cloud bird in her hands and plucking the wings from it to shape it into a flower. "No more animal clouds today. That is for another day."

Amon frowned.

"Come on Daxton," Madame Flintridge said.

Daxton stood up and walked over to where Catherine was, ready to sit on the empty cloud beside her, until it moved from its position to right across from her.

"Sit," Catherine said.

Daxton didn't know if it was his own action or the air around him that caused him to sit, but he did so very quickly. He looked at Catherine's posture and was sure she was sterner than Theresa.

Catherine displayed her array, which wasn't just one in the center but six; one small array for each finger and then a larger circle in the center. She flicked her pinky until all the circles merged in the center. He felt his cloud chair shift.

"You're Jessica and Zoey's friend, right?" Daxton asked.

"Don't speak to me," Catherine snarled.

What?

"You don't get it," Catherine said, cutting him off. "I was lucky that the Elemental Order even allowed me to come because of my family history and I just can't be associated with you at all. I can't look different or weird or weak."

"How does being associated with me make you any of that?" Daxton asked.

Daxton watched as Catherine spelled out her name with her finger, Catherine Marie de' Medici Drake Tanner.

Daxton's eyes went wide, reading her name displayed in the clouds. This was the first time he had seen anyone ever with his last name. Even though Pat had named him when he was a baby, she said she had read it on a note that Thelma denied ever existed, countering that he was named after a great uncle of hers. "How do you know my last name? Are we related?"

Her nostrils flared and her eyes blazed. She looked at him like he had five heads. He leaned back, afraid of what she might do.

"No! I have no association with the name Tanner and if you were smart neither would you," Catherine whispered, glaring at him.

"They didn't call you 'Tanner' at the ceremony," Daxton said.

"That's because I am registered under my mother's name," Catherine said.

"Madame Theresa didn't say anything about Tanners being here or that they were bad."

Why wouldn't she tell me something like that?

"Yeah? Why do you think that is?" Catherine said.

"I don't know." He scrunched his eyebrows in thought, but no answer came to him. "But how do you know my last name," Daxton asked again.

"You're not stupid, are you?" Catherine asked.

"No," Daxton said, trying not to sound offended.

"Well, I'm not either," Catherine stated, her eyes cast down to her broach. "They hid your name at the ceremony. There had to be a reason for that; no one would dare come back here using the name Tanner. Now, no more questions."

"Fine. Just show me how you do that with your array, and I can go back to my seat," Daxton said.

"You can't just be shown this, it has to evolve over time," Catherine said.

Daxton was distracted by her disgust at their last name.

Why would they hide my name? What hasn't Theresa told me?

As much as he wanted to think about it, he couldn't. Not while in class. He mimicked what Catherine did with her hands, joining them together and separating them in hopes to split his array. No matter how hard he concentrated, he couldn't do it. He grew so mad, as she was easily able to make hers into six.

"You're not concentrating!" Catherine yelled.

"Yes, I am! Daxton yelled back as a black cloud formed above his head. He saw his array barely dividing as the cloud grew, followed by the roar of thunder

The cloud moved up and over to Halo's purple cloud and absorbed it. In shock, Daxton watched the cloud turn green and then little, green frogs began to fall from it. One jumped on his cloud desk and smiled at him before hopping away. His mind did a double take as everyone around him started to scream.

"HALO!" Madame Flintridge yelled, spinning around while holding out her hand as a green frog flopped into it!

Large drops of water began to fall from the black cloud above Halo's head. "Thanks for your help," Daxton said to Catherine as he stood.

"Avoid me," Catherine ordered, leaving the room.

Rude!

"Halo!" Madame Flintridge yelled again, struggling to unfold an umbrella. "What did you do?"

"I didn't do it!" Halo replied in confusion as a frog jumped onto her head.

The gongs rang for the next class. Bjorn and Ivan grabbed Daxton, opened the cloud door, and rushed into the hall.

"Boys! You get back here!" Madame Flintridge yelled again, as the frogs continued to fall from the shrinking cloud.

"What was that?" Bjorn asked once they were down the hall.

"I don't know," Daxton said, rubbing his head. Hearing footsteps behind him, he turned around to find Sengal standing there with a broom in his hand.

"What did you do?" Sengal asked, looking at the growing mess of frogs.

"If I knew what I did or what I'm doing I would have stopped it. How was I supposed to know this was going to happen?"

"Don't you know how to control your power?" Sengal asked.

This was a question that took Daxton's mind for a loop.

No, I don't.

"Why do you kids always do this?" Sengal asked. He sighed and snapped his fingers. Plants appeared that ate the frogs.

"It's not his fault," Iris said, walking up to the pair.

Iris looped Daxton's arm and pulled him with her as Sengal stared. "Let's go. It's time for our independent study," Iris said.

"Independent study?" Daxton responded.

"Yeah, in the mornings we have class and then we can go practice what we learned or go study. Whatever we need to do to help ourselves grow.."

Iris and Daxton talked more about different things from the Normal Lands. It sounded so different in the Sky Dome than it did back home. The Normal Lands were full of noises that didn't exist here, like car horns or airplanes flying overhead. He was glad to have someone to talk to that had at least been there; he didn't feel as much like a loner anymore. Part of him wished he didn't have his array so he could be in class with Brent and Tiffany.

Daxton told Iris he would see her later. He wanted a few moments alone to check on Brea and Blaze, so he moved down the hall to the boys' bathroom and checked to make sure it was empty.

The bathroom was bigger than he expected, with a volcano in the center that let out water instead of fire. Moving over to the counter, he opened his satchel and out popped Brea's little white head, chirping as she stretched her cloud wings and flew about. Before too long, Blaze also came out. Daxton laughed watching the two before quickly calling them back. They responded by giving him a sad look, but they still came to him.

"I know, but I have to keep you safe," Daxton said, helping them back into the satchel. Making his way back to the central dome, he heard footsteps and his hand went to his satchel. Madame Flintridge and Madame Theresa came to a halt in the hall. They seemed to be having a serious conversation. Earlier, he had heard Halo talking from across the room and he wondered if he could do it again. Moving his right hand over to his right ear, he touched the lobe. At first, he just heard a loud noise, then he took both hands and held one over each ear and the noise lessened and he could hear Madame Theresa's voice.

"Maybe so," Madame Theresa said.

"Is the rumor true? Did some of the students see something? Eleagons?" Madame Flintridge asked.

Daxton could see the uncomfortable look on Theresa's face from his spot down the hall.

"They are just hatchlings and, well, I am sure any rumors you heard should be put to bed," Madame Theresa answered, but not with much confidence.

"Of course, but you should have told me the moment you found out. I was barely able to control myself when I saw the air one on Daxton's desk."

"I did tell you," Theresa argued. "I sent an Obble."

"I never got one," Madame Flintridge said.

"Odd," Theresa said, rubbing her forehead.

"Yes, odd indeed. And he has two eleagons?"

Daxton froze.

"Yes, an air one and a fire one," Madame Theresa said. "I saw them protect the children, so we have nothing to fear right now. Are you worried for their safety?"

"Of course, I am," Madame Flintridge said, looking directly into her eyes. "Hopefully the children will be more understanding about this."

"Hopefully, and about the children," Madame Theresa said, changing the subject. "I knew Raizy was going to have to take Darkness this year, but I didn't expect them all to have to take it. I sent an obble to the council to appeal this."

"Theresa, you know appealing could take weeks or months; they are to start the class this week," Madame Flintridge said in a worried tone.

"Well, I will just have to send lots of obbles until I get in to see them. Do you know why Vulkan hired him?" she asked.

"No, I don't know why Vulkan insisted on him. Something about needing him to help stabilize the Tree," Madame Flintridge answered.

"Vulkan knows exactly how to stabilize the Eternal Tree. It has not been a problem for years. Why does he need help now?" Madame Theresa asked.

"I don't know, but it's not like we have much of an option," Madame Flintridge whispered.

"Well, wait until I can find out more. I mean he might want to use the air eleagon to stabilize the tree if he can't use one of the arrays. But I still don't want the eleagons to be seen."

Daxton's hand went straight to his satchel.

Use Brea? I don't care if Vulkan needed her to cool off a glass of lemonade, he would never get his greedy little hands on her or Blaze.

Looking around cautiously, he wondered if he should have listened to Theresa's warning about keeping them in his room.

Surely, they are safer with me than alone in my room. Could they really be in danger?

CHAPTER 12 – HOROLOGY

The next day, Daxton woke up peacefully, the weirdness of yesterday behind him. There was a lot he still had to learn about this place, but he would need to take it one day at a time.

He got dressed and then looked at his eleagons. They glanced up at him expectantly.

I know I'm supposed to leave them here, but how can I know they're safe?

Before he could decide about leaving them or bringing them, they jumped into his satchel.

Today he had horology. He wasn't exactly sure what that was, but Iris told him that she heard it was pretty boring.

Time to find out if she's right.

Daxton reached the stairs made from gears that led to the Observatory Clock Tower. Once up this staircase, there was a long hallway made of large broken clock pieces. Daxton felt like he was walking through a clock. Reaching the gear door, he pushed it open, his fingers trembling from excitement. There were several desks made of gears and walls covered with every type of clock imaginable: sundials, grandfather clocks, watches. It was amazing. Out from behind a gear desk stood a very short man with a big belly and only a few gray hairs.

Daxton looked around and saw Brent and Tiffany before also noticing Zoey, Halo, Bjorn, Amon, Jessica, Valerie, and Nicholas. With a smile, Daxton sat between Brent and Tiffany.

"I didn't know we'd be in the same class," Daxton said.

"Yeah, with the level zero stuff, I didn't know if we would see each other in any of our classes," Brent said.

Bjorn leaned toward them. "It's because there are some classes that don't need arrays, so we can all take them no matter our levels."

Daxton nodded, happy he could take some classes with his friends.

"Welcome, amateurs," the man announced in a husky voice, pushing his half-moon spectacles up on his pointy nose. Small, blue eyes hid behind them. Daxton was taken aback by this teacher calling everyone an amateur, but he realized the man was just trying to break the ice, even if it was obviously awkward.

"My name is Mr. Hopkins," he said, looking around the room. "I am a horologist, one who studies time." Moving down the aisle, he gestured with his hand at the wide collection of clocks. "Clocks keep time. It is how we know when we are late. Tardiness is unacceptable. I suggest at least one of you needs a new timepiece." He stared at Daxton with a semi-stern look. Breaking into a smile almost immediately, he gave up pretending to be serious and broke into a giggle.

Mr. Hopkins weaved his way through the gear desks. There was a friendliness about him that Daxton really liked.

Halo leaned over to Zoey and whispered in her ear, "Did you see Daxton in class yesterday? I never knew anyone from the No Lands could do that."

"I know. Shocking," Zoey said.

Daxton heard them and turned red with embarrassment. Despite that, a smile of pride crept over his face.

"Halo, Zoey," Mr. Hopkins said, scratching the bridge of his nose, "I will not tolerate any gossip in this room." He turned to the front of the class. "If you are curious about Daxton," he added, looking right at Daxton, "just ask him."

Daxton blinked and looked over to Halo and Zoey.

Did Mr. Hopkins also have the ability to improve his own hearing or had the two girls been too loud?

He glanced to see how far away Mr. Hopkins was.

"Ah!" Mr. Hopkins nodded, turning the gears on the wall clock. "I can hear every sound in the room," he stated proudly, picking up little glass jars.

Making his way around the room, he handed everyone a small glass of water, a cork, and a straight piece of metal. "All right," he instructed. "This is a basic navigation tool that can help you find your way. This class will always be filled with riddles and puzzles for you to solve," he said, smiling. "All you really need is time."

He moved back to his desk, turned to a section of the wall where there were many small globes with gears, and flipped the gears until letters appeared.

"Oh!" Mr. Hopkins paused with a twinkle in his eyes. "This is the answer to your puzzle." The gears formed letters, which formed words. Daxton read, *Sometimes a key opens an unknown lock.*

"In advanced classes, you will learn how to see through time and how objects around you tell you what to expect before it happens," Mr. Hopkins said, growing excited. "Objects can hold time. By placing your hand on an object, you may be able to go back to see an important event." Mr. Hopkins walked toward the door, placing his hand on the knob, and looking over at his classroom. "You will not do any of that today. Today, your task is to exit this room in a matter of fifty minutes using the items I've given you. Your time begins now."

The classroom erupted into gasps and mumbles.

"Oh, and to make things more exciting, a hurricane will form when time is up! Better hurry." The instructor cracked a smile before opening the door and leaving. A *clank* was heard as he bolted the door from the outside.

"He's crazy!" Tiffany yelled, running to the door to see if she could open it. She banged and pulled on it, but it was locked. The noise of the children talking became louder as they started to panic.

"He left us in this room without a way out!" Zoey shrieked, visibly alarmed.

"Well, he couldn't leave us without a way out," Amon countered.

"Yeah," Nicholas chimed in. "I mean, he left us water, a cork, and this metal thing. It must do something."

Brent tried to pull the door open himself. "Yep," Brent stated. "We're locked in."

Tiffany hit him on the head. "That's what I said! We've wasted another minute because of your brilliant observation, Brent." Without warning, a light gust wafted throughout the room and Tiffany began to panic. "It's starting. We're going to die! I want to go home!"

"No one is going to die," Daxton interjected. "It's a riddle. We have to figure it out." He scanned the room for any sign of a clue. Counting the students, he shared, "There are twelve of us, like a clock." He looked at the clear water in the glass on his desk and picked up the cork. Knowing that it would float, he dropped it in the water. "Everyone, look at your water and metal piece. See if you can make it do something."

One of the clocks ticked; another minute gone.

The students fiddled and studied their water. Amon put the glass on his head. Zoey stirred it with her finger. Nicholas drank a sip of his and said, "Yep, water." Brent stared at his glass.

"This is stupid," Tiffany huffed as the clock ticked again and the force of the breeze increased. She picked up her piece of metal and then set it back down. Her long, blonde hair fell and rubbed against it, generating a small amount of static. She picked up the metal again and dropped it in the water. As it sank, it began to spin. "Daxton!" yelled Tiffany. "Mine moved!"

"What?" asked Brent, looking over at her in amazement.

Tiffany picked up her glass of water and walked over to Daxton. Her needle struggled to move on the bottom of the cup as she watched with a smile on her face.

"The needle is trying to move, but it can't because the bottom of the cup is rough," Daxton said and took out the needle. After dropping it in the cup again, he watched it turn as it fell to the bottom where it tried to continue moving but couldn't.

"It's like a compass!" Brent shouted, watching it move. "If the metal could float, it just might work! What did you use to magnetize the needle?"

"Magnetize?" asked Tiffany in confusion.

"You know, static electricity," Brent clarified.

"Nothing," Tiffany answered as she hopped up and down. "In your face," she gloated, holding the cup victoriously over her head. "The late bloomers can do it." She twirled back to her seat.

"Nope," Brent said, slowly placing his needle in the water. It didn't move, instead it sank uselessly. "You used something to get it started, but it doesn't work properly just yet. We could use the cork to make the needle float."

"I didn't use anything," Tiffany snapped, glaring at Brent.

"No need to argue. We can figure it out," Daxton instructed, hearing the clock ding loudly as the winds picked up. He knew they didn't have time for bickering.

With the sound of a thunderclap, rain began to fall in the room.

Tiffany grimaced but took her needle out and laid it on the desk.

Brent pondered a moment before rubbing his needle on his clothes. He placed it on the desk where it tried to move. Excited, he stuck it through the cork and placed it in the water. As he suspected, it began to spin. "Everyone, rub the metal on your clothes, put it through the cork, then place it in the water."

Everyone did as instructed,

"Now go where it points," commanded Brent.

The students wandered around the room, holding their glasses of water as the metal pieces pointed, leading everyone in a different direction. The flurries of air inside the classroom became more powerful.

"Here!" Tiffany yelled, her needle pointing at an orrery clock, which was a mechanical model of the solar system with planets and moons. There was a ring around Neptune that did not belong there. "Here!" Tiffany repeated, "this ring is rougher, a weird metal or something."

Ivan and Bjorn found their gears with ease. Nicholas was busy moving clocks around to find his piece before the rising water obscured the smaller dial clock, which had a jagged edge that was severely out of place. He grabbed it quickly and went to Ivan and Bjorn.

Amon found an extra gear on one of the clocks and removed it, knowing he had made the right move when the clock continued working without a hitch. Everyone but Daxton found similar items that were out of place, made from peculiar materials, or had uneven edges. They laid them on the front desk and looked at one another with uncertainty.

"Okay, now what?" asked Amon.

"Give it to Brent," Tiffany answered. "He can put anything together."

"Yeah, I am the master at this stuff," Brent replied, fiddling with the pieces. Cogs and gears seamlessly fit together, and Brent grew more excited as he saw where the gears belonged. He placed each one on top of the other.

The room was suddenly lit by a flash of light, followed immediately by a deafening boom of thunder, making everyone jump. The water was knee-high already and the wind continued to increase, blowing all loose papers around the room.

Daxton frantically ran around the room following the needle of his compass. Each time he got to a spot, the needle changed direction. Finally, Daxton looked up when the needle changed direction. High up in the rafters, between some ironworks, he located a piece of metal with ridges. With no way to reach it, Daxton looked around for a ladder, but there wasn't one to be found. Instead, he pulled a desk over, and then another, and another, stacking them one on top of one another to build a makeshift ladder.

Daxton took his first step before climbing to the top of the desks. The piece of metal was wedged between two folding ironworks and appeared to be out of place. Daxton knew this was his piece and his heart raced as the winds picked up again, threatening to blow Daxton and the makeshift ladder down. He stretched his hand out for the piece, but it was several inches beyond his reach.

There is no time to climb down and rebuild the ladder closer.

"Hurry, Daxton!" Amon yelled over the howling wind.

"We need the last piece!" Bjorn bellowed.

"If you can't get it, get out of the way and I can do it!" Catherine fussed.

"You can do it, Daxton, just think PINK!" Halo yelled, raising her fist.

I can do this. I can show everyone that I am not worthless. All I need to do is get this one piece.

Daxton closed his eyes and concentrated. As he did, the boy heard nothing but his own breath and the thundering of his heart. The wind pounded against him, within another few minutes it was all going to be over. Each of them would be sucked up into a hurricane.

It was like time was standing still. He thought he could hear his classmates calling for him, but all sounds were a dull thrum. Everything was in slow motion while he tried to make a decision. The stinging rain hit his face as the room continued to fill with water.

Keeping his eyes tightly shut, Daxton thrust his hand as far as it would go, but he still could not reach the piece. Frustration and anger started to take over, but the young student remembered Raizey telling him that he had to control his emotions to control his powers.

That's it.

He took a deep breath and concentrated, reaching out not only with his hand but also his mind, allowing his fear and panic to fade away.

Daxton's array illuminated and the piece floated into his outstretched hand. Feeling the cool triangular metal, Daxton opened his eyes with a smile before quickly scrambling down the stack of desks.

"Hurry, Daxton!" called Tiffany in a panic over the roaring wind. "I don't want to drown in here!"

Daxton ran to Brent and handed him the final piece of the puzzle, feeling pride as he watched the piece fit to form a key from the parts that Brent assembled. Brent hurried to the door and put the key in the doorknob, but it would not turn. At that same moment, a surge of water poured from the ceiling and pushed Brent to the back of the room, forcing him to drop the key. Tiffany floated by, trying to swim. Daxton, who had scrambled up a bookcase in fear, held out his hand, grabbed her, and pulled her to the bookshelf.

"Where's the key?" Daxton asked frantically.

"Brent has it," Tiffany hollered over the pounding winds.

She started climbing away. "I'm going to look for Brent!"

The wind howled like a savage beast crying out with massive, unyielding raw power. Daxton knew what he needed to do, but he hesitated. He could not bring himself to dive into the water. Everyone was going to die because Daxton could not overcome his fear of water to get the key.

Suddenly, Brea was next to Daxton, plunging into the water. The little eleagon formed a bubble of air around herself as she fought her way to the bottom, dodging clocks that floated to the top. Finally, Brea popped up out of the water, proudly holding the key in her mouth. Daxton was close enough to the door that he stuck the key into the lock.

The door unlocked and a wave of children were swept out of the room and into the hallway.

Daxton sat in a puddle of water, spotting Blaze on the ground. He bent down and picked him up. The eleagon looked like he was going to vomit; Blaze hated water.

"He better not vomit on me," said Tiffany, who was lying next to Daxton.

"You won't vomit on Tiffany, will you?" Daxton asked, still trying to make out what happened while watching Brea return to the satchel.

Mr. Hopkins appeared, looking at his pocket watch. He clapped his hands. "Well done, well done indeed. See what happens when we work together? A key can be more than just a piece of metal used to unlock a chest or door. It can also be a key to understanding and a means of unlocking the truth. Like an answer to an unknown question, sometimes a key opens an unknown lock. Time for lunch. I will see all of you next week; or will I?" He smiled before walking away.

Daxton was dumbfounded and wanted to shout at Mr. Hopkins but remained quiet.

"I am not going to see him next week or any other day," Zoey huffed.

"That was, uh, interesting," Brent mumbled, pushing himself up. "He did mention lunch, though. And I like lunch."

"Yeah, you would almost die and then worry about food," Tiffany replied. "You're still a weirdo." She squeezed the water from her hair.

"I am not," Brent retorted, helping Zoey stand. "Daxton's piece was the primary one I needed. His piece held it all together. That was amazing of you, Daxton, to get the key from under the water after I dropped it." Brent looked away sheepishly, "Sorry about that, by the way."

"Yeah," said Tiffany, who was the only person aware of Daxton's fear of water. "You are so brave."

"Daxton, how were you able to get your piece down?" Zoey asked.

"I called to it and it was like it was waiting on me," Daxton answered, holding up the gear key, not acknowledging that he did not actually recover the key.

"Not bad for a kid from the No Lands. Think it can open anything else?" asked Amon.

Daxton shook the water from his hair. "I don't have a clue."

"I vote that the key has a place with you," Nicholas advised.

"No, Brent ought to have it," Daxton rebutted.

"It didn't work for me," Brent said. "I mean, the moment I tried to turn it, that gigantic rush of water fell on us. The key was meant for you, Daxton. And no offense, I don't think I want to hang on to whatever it can do."

All the children agreed with Brent.

"Actually," Brent interjected, "I think it really is meant for you."

"What do you mean?" Daxton asked.

"Look at the key; the end matches your pendant."

Sure enough, Brent was right. Daxton's piece of the key looked just like his pendant. The triangle of the key was a perfect match, and when he brought the two together, they both glowed for a moment, before dimming back together. They were meant to be together.

The students began to illuminate their arrays, drying themselves from the first task. Ivan used his array to direct air at Daxton, Tiffany, and Brent, drying their robes and hair.

Daxton smiled as his pendant flew upwards from the force of the air and rubbed his thumb across the key.

What else do you open?

CHAPTER 13 - MORE OBBLES

On Wednesday morning, Daxton was excited for his array class. Stepping through the archway to enter the large classroom, he found it filled with several three-dimensional shapes.

What's the story with each shape?

As his eyes wandered the large area, he saw Halo, Zoey, and Catherine talking in the center of the room, and Amon and Nicholas by the bookshelves reading a blue book.

"Take a seat," Madame Theresa instructed as she walked in, flipping her wrist, and illuminating her purple array. "The most important aspect of your array is the many shapes it will produce. No two arrays are alike," she said, looking out at her class. "Please work on your hand gestures during your independent study. Stand and let's practice."

Hand gestures?

Daxton stood up.

Theresa instructed the class to stand in a large circle. As soon as they did, the cloud desks became smaller and moved up into the ceiling, giving the children enough space to practice. Theresa stood in the center of the circle so she could observe everyone easily.

"You're going to stand with your shoulders back. Good. Now put your palms out. As your array forms, you can use the center finger on your other hand to make your array as big as you want or need. Allow me to demonstrate."

Theresa, in the middle of the circle, held out her own palm. Quickly, her array began to glow purple, silver, and white. Using her other hand, the array grew bigger and bigger until it surrounded her. Daxton could hardly see her through her own array. Soon, the array shrank and was just a small circle in her hand. She looked around, and then at her palm. What was just a circle became a cone, and then a cube. With a flick of her wrist, it all disappeared.

"See how much your array can be?"

The class looked at her with wide eyes.

That's what we're going to learn? That's so cool!

"Now go ahead and try. I'll guide you as needed."

For the rest of class, Daxton practiced illuminating his array on command. Madame Theresa came around often to offer words of encouragement and instruction, but Daxton had very little luck in activating his array. As his frustration grew, he shouted in anger, causing his array to appear for a moment and a gust of wind to extend from him out into the room ahead, knocking Amon to the ground.

The students all stared at Daxton.

Madame Theresa made an announcement as she checked on Amon. "Everyone, back to practicing. I have a special treat for you after class."

As the class resumed, Madame Theresa, convinced that Amon was okay, approached Daxton and sternly whispered to him. "Daxton, you must control your emotions. You could hurt someone."

Daxton looked up at Madame Theresa, still excited from the feel of the power that had flowed through him. He did not want to listen; he wanted to feel the power again, but the word 'hurt' got to him and he looked over at Amon. "I am sorry Amon," apologized Daxton. "I didn't mean for that to happen."

"It is okay. I know you didn't mean to." Amon looked sincere, but he also looked afraid.

As the students continued practicing, the room looked like a laser light show with the glow of many arrays bouncing around one another. Daxton spent the rest of the class in thought. It wasn't long until the gongs rang out signaling the end of class. The students all looked to Madame Theresa in anticipation of their promised surprise.

"Now, I know everyone is excited to practice what you have learned, so instead of leaving class for you to practice on your own, I have arranged for you to practice against another society." Madame Theresa nodded and continued as students entered from the hallway. "You will have a battle of strength and will. Water versus air. Student versus student."

"What do you mean by battle?" Amon asked nervously.

"Just that," Madame Theresa responded, as several students from the Aquaious Society entered the class. "The aqua students will try to get the air students wet. The air students need only stay dry until I say stop or you get your opponent wet. Best two out of three wins."

Daxton thought about the rules. He just had to stay dry.

Air is all around us, but water vapor is often found mixed with the air. Water elementors could use the water in the air unless the humidity was so low there was not enough water in the air. That is their weakness. I don't think the room is humid enough for them to make much water. This should be easy if I can get my array to activate.

Daxton lined up on the end of the line of Aeroious students and watched as Aquaious students assumed their positions across from them. Daxton was somewhat relieved when the last one lined up across from Halo, leaving him without an opponent. A clearing of a throat caused Daxton to turn and see standing face-to-face with him, the little sister of the self-proclaimed future of Eldragor. Blair Luxador smiled.

Apprehension washed over Daxton, but at least he knew her weakness to be lack of water.

Then Madame Theresa placed a large bowl of water at the feet of each Aquaious student.

So much for their weakness.

"Position and form," called out Madame Theresa.

Everyone took their position with palms up and illuminated their arrays. Blue and purple shapes danced on the walls. Daxton concentrated on his palm and willed his array to appear. It did not.

"Ready, begin!" shouted Theresa.

Blair illuminated her blue array further and pulled the water from the glass, making it bend to her will. She chuckled in delight when she saw Daxton had no array. "Someone is about to get wet," she giggled and moved her array and thus a ball of water towards the defenseless boy.

Afraid of the water and possible humiliation, Daxton panicked. Without warning, his array appeared, and Daxton watched a tiny cyclone leap from his array towards the water ball that floated towards him. The spinning air blew Blair's water all around the room with ease. Daxton smiled for a moment until he noticed the smile on Blair's face.

Why is she smiling? I destroyed her beam of water.

"Point for Blair! Daxton is wet," called out Madame Theresa.

Oh. I forgot the rules. I got wet.

"Daxton, I assume you just learned that power does not always equate to victory," stated Madame Theresa sternly before calling out, "Lilly is wet!"

"No," Lily cried out as a wave of water overcame her wall of wind. "The only thing I hate worse than losing is getting wet."

Daxton was so distraught that he was not aware of other results, knowing only that both he and Lily were wet. As he prepared for Blair's next assault, Daxton dared not even glance around the room for fear of losing concentration and thus his array.

153

"Remember, best two out of three," announced Theresa as the pairs prepared to battle again. "Ready, begin."

This time Daxton was smarter in his use of his array and put up a wall of wind that easily blocked Blairs water beam and blew the water all over Blair, whose face drew into a snarl.

"Oh, we have a battle here," announced Theresa. Apparently, the other pairs were lopsided, and all finished two to nothing. "Everyone except Blair and Daxton line up against a new opponent. Losers versus losers and winners versus winners. Ready, begin."

Not at all happy about the last result, Blair pulled all the water from her cup and forced it at Daxton's wall. As the water threatened to go over, under, and around Daxton's wall, his wall expanded ahead of the water, keeping Daxton dry. Blair yelled out in rage.

By now, the other student battles had ended. Blair pulled all the water in the room into her array. With a snarl, she sent a wave up towards the ceiling and then down towards Daxton's head. As the wave crashed over him, Daxton's array simply continued to expand the air wall and formed a bubble around the young elementor. The water crashed down around the bubble and washed across the floor, getting everyone else's feet wet, including Blairs, but Daxton stayed dry.

A huge smile washed over Daxton's face.

I won. I beat a Luxador.

Daxton had no idea the outcomes of the other battles, only that he had won.

"Daxton, you won. You beat Blair" Halo called out in excitement and shock.

"Great job," Madame Theresa stated with approval. "Aeroious wins. You are all free to go."

"Well done, Daxton," Theresa whispered, smiling at him.

Daxton returned the smile with his array still illuminated. He didn't want to extinguish his array as he left the class, so he concentrated on keeping it illuminated as he hurried out of class and stumbled straight into Ambassador Vulkan.

"Watch where you're going," Ambassador Vulkan barked, entering Theresa's room. "And be careful with your array."

Daxton grew angry that Vulkan had caused him to lose concentration and his array to go out. As he turned to say something to Vulkan, he realized that would be unwise. Trying to control his emotions, Daxton turned to walk away, but heard Vulkan's voice from inside Theresa's classroom.

"What is it, woman?" Vulkan demanded in a harsh tone. "If you send me one more of those obbles that blast around my head, I will find a way to make sure that they will not be delivered anymore."

"Then you should respond when I need you," Theresa said.

"What is it?" Vulkan asked.

"You know darn well why I need to see you. How could you? I knew there was an ulterior motive to you bringing Morpheus here. If you want to have him teach advanced students, fine, but the others should not take Darkness."

"Theresa, it has been decided that all students will be taking Darkness this year," Vulkan retorted. "Whatever issue you have with Morpheus will have to wait. I need a teacher and he is the best one to do the job."

"It is impossible. They are not strong enough and may not be safe. They could hurt themselves. He might even hurt them."

"Oh, please, Theresa. Do you hear yourself? I would never allow harm to come to any of the students. Morpheus's teachings are a bit extreme, I admit, but I do hope we can determine the weak ones much quicker. This will also provide the rest with a way to better protect themselves."

"Much quicker than eight weeks? You must mean overnight." Theresa extorted. Daxton imagined her shaking her head disapprovingly. "I will appeal to the Council."

"I oversee the Eternal Tree and will use whatever means necessary to keep us from going extinct, even if it means we have to teach a little bit about Darkness. I have learned much from Morpheus and I suggest you and the other teachers take the opportunity to learn as well. You may not believe me, but that class will help protect these students."

"And what of the ones who can't be protected through this?"

"Like I said, we will determine the students who cannot handle it here, and if history serves us well, your kind will be the ones that won't be able to handle it."

Your kind?

Daxton watched Ambassador Vulkan storm out of the classroom, and then glanced at his palm. His array began to glow.

We aren't as weak as you think we are.

CHAPTER 14 - TERERBIS

When Daxton woke up, he noticed a sense of dread coming over himself while preparing for class: Darkness.

Why shouldn't we take it? It's not like I'm going to be taught how to raise the dead. I don't want to be seen as weak, and this could make me stronger.

Daxton shook himself out of his thoughts and grabbed his map, which was printed on the back of the schedule, from his satchel to locate where the Darkness class would be. He looked up at Brent, who was sipping some of his antiuum brewtion. "We need to go to the northwest area to the Terra Tower of Way," Daxton said.

Daxton couldn't help but think about what this class would really offer.

Could it really be as terrible as Madame Theresa thinks?

Soon, they were at the Tower of Way. Once inside, they came to an open door on the left. Daxton stood in the doorway under an arch, looking in to see if this was the right place. He was hoping there would be something like a sign, or anything to give him some information. To his dismay, the room was dark and gloomy, and Daxton found it very difficult to see until his eyes adjusted to the darkness.

"Don't just stand there," a voice rang out from the dimly lit room. "You may enter, but do so quietly."

With a gulp, Daxton crossed over the threshold and Brent followed. Stale, cold air filled his lungs as he looked at the source of the voice sitting on a large, black throne. Swirling a red liquid in an etched silver goblet, the man on the throne was tall and lanky. His dark, shiny hair matched his robes. It was like he was darkness himself.

Aside from the throne upon which the man sat, there were no chairs.

Are we supposed to stand the whole class?

The dark walls had gothic stone arches and candles in chandeliers that illuminated only the front half of the room. There were bookcases stationed around the room, and cages hanging from the rafters containing skeletons of birds. In the far left corner was a narrow, black iron staircase spiraling upward to a balcony that had a door leading to another room. It was like a nightmare coming to life.

Brent and Daxton found Tiffany standing by a bookcase, scanning the titles of books, and walked over to her.

"Have you been taking the antiuum?" Brent whispered.

"Yes. I take it when I wake up," Tiffany said, taking her hand to a book labeled 'Shadow Beast.'

Morpheus cleared his throat and Daxton watched as Morpheus moved his hand outward and flicked his wrist, causing a black array to appear. The children had no willpower as their legs forced them to take a seat on the dusty, black stone floor. All except Daxton.

Morpheus's smile grew into an evil grin as he turned and saw the boy. He stared silently for a moment as Daxton stood there before standing and walking to Daxton. He looked the child up and down and then walked around behind him.

Daxton felt Morpheus breathing down his neck as the other children all sat around in silence. He wanted to just disappear. A coldness moved through him and the only thing he felt was his pendant warm on his chest.

"Very interesting. But I would sit down if I were you, Daxton," Morpheus taunted. The teacher leaned in close and whispered, "Before others begin to think you are not what they think you are."

Daxton froze. No other teacher had called him out like this. As his anger began to rise, his array illuminated.

"I am Master Morpheus Valdor," the teacher said as he regained his throne and then snapped his fingers. Almost immediately, the children were released from the man's hold.

Next to Daxton, Brent stood up again and gingerly touched Daxton's shoulder. With his friend's guidance, Daxton extinguished his array and sat on the floor with the others.

"And you already know your classmate, Daxton Tanner."

After what Catherine told Daxton on Monday, he wanted to fall through the floor.

This can't be good!

He began hearing the rumblings from his fellow classmates and, glancing around, saw a mix of disgust and pity. Catherine looked like she was barely able to hold it together.

"A Tanner! Here!" a student called out angrily.

"Hush now children, it gets better," Morpheus said, mockingly.

What could be worse than this?

"Release them!" Morpheus said, rising from his throne.

Daxton moved his hand to his satchel on instinct and took a deep breath. As far as he knew, only a few people were aware of his eleagons, and he wasn't about to make it known to everyone that he had them. He stared back at Morpheus.

Why didn't I leave them in the room?

"RELEASE THEM, I order!" Morpheus commanded again. The man's voice was louder than Daxton thought possible before.

Before Daxton could think of what to do, the top of his satchel flapped open, and out flew Brea and Blaze.

Morpheus's face twisted into a dark smile and his eyes lit up.

Daxton's eyes grew wide. He lifted his hand, and a thin veil of smoke and fire surrounded his palm. "BREA! BLAZE!" Daxton called and his face grew hot hearing the whispers behind him.

"So, they have names," Morpheus said, his left palm up. He couldn't stop staring at them as they flew around, making Daxton nervous. "Would they come to me if I called them? Brea. Blaze," Morpheus asked in a mocking tone. A black mist spread from the center of Morpheus's palm as the man tried to contact the eleagons.

Brea and Blaze, however, ignored him and continued to circle above Daxton.

"They're bonded to you. That is most unfortunate," Morpheus said, curling his hand in. The black mist dissipated.

"What does that mean?" Daxton asked, furrowing his brows.

"It means the only way for anyone else to control them is for you to die."

He'd heard this before, but being told this news by the man in front of him made it feel much direr. For the first time, Daxton felt a strange sense of danger and of impending doom.

"Did you think you would be able to hide them? The boy with the answers; the boy with the eleagons. You can never hide the truth, no matter how hard you try."

The whispers around Daxton grew louder as Brea landed on one shoulder and Blaze on the other. He couldn't turn back now; his secrets were out. With a heavy stomach his face grew hot.

"For the next few weeks, I will be instructing you on the use of dark manipulation," Morpheus said, changing the subject. "Daxton, define dream walking."

Daxton didn't have the answer. He sat, lips closed tight, trying to avoid eye contact.

"Useless!" Morpheus sighed.

Daxton wanted to shrink even more than he had before. This class was never going to go well for him; he could feel it.

"Amon, define dream walking."

"It's, um, visiting the dreams of another," he said, voice shaking.

"Can one be harmed?" Morpheus asked, glancing around the class.

"My dad said his brother was killed in a dream," Iris whispered.

"Yes, one can be hurt like that. You can also lose control of yourself. Learn to build a wall, so you are not made to be a puppet. Today you will practice that. You will continue to practice it in your independent study today. I know other teachers will let you work on other things during their independent study days, but I will not. I can tell if you are slacking off, and this is one of the most important things you can learn. Ever since the Rift, it has been easier for dreams to be invaded. You cannot let the darkness win. Let's begin."

They spent the next hour working, studying, and practicing. The students needed to be able to visualize energy to put a mental shield up. Morpheus told them that the key to this, especially at their young age, was meditation. It would be difficult to close their eyes and visualize something that could truly protect them. It was enough to think of a shield to start. They needed to believe in it with their whole body.

Daxton tried to concentrate, but when he closed his eyes, all he saw was darkness. He sighed in frustration.

"When you go to bed tonight," Morpheus started, "close your eyes and open your mind. Think of something you can take with you into your dreams. It will be difficult, but do this every night."

Taking something with you. What could I take with me?

Daxton looked down at Brea and Blaze, a small smile dancing on his lips. He closed his eyes and saw them for just a moment, playing like the first night he had them. Their small blue and red bodies zoomed by him, taking turns chasing each other. They moved faster than he'd ever seen, but then they stopped, almost frozen. A darkness began to swirl in his mind, overtaking them. A beast flashed in his vision, and before he could do anything, Brea and Blaze were gone. His eyes sprung open, and he was back in class.

It was only a dream, right? Right?

Seeing the eleagons, he was somewhat comforted.

The ringing of gongs echoed all around, signaling the end of class. Daxton was exhausted. He caught stares while walking out. His hand went to the pendant on his chest as Morpheus's words played over in his head.

You are not what they think you are.

CHAPTER 15 – BREWTION

Finally, it was Friday. Even at a training academy like Eldragor, Daxton couldn't help but be excited for the weekend. He just had one more class to go. Looking across his room, he noticed Brent was gone.

Did he already go to class?

Daxton walked from the northwest area to the north tower, noticing how the area changed to nature scenes; even the floor was now grass and not stone.

Did I just walk outside again?

He got his map and syllabus out making sure he read B101 and was headed in the right direction. Hanging from the limbs were letters and numbers, signifying the classes. He looked up when he heard footsteps.

"The mural is beautiful, just like the outside used to be," Halo said, stepping to the side of him.

"How do they make this look so real?" Daxton asked.

"Terra people work best when enveloped in a natural environment, so they use elemental paints made to look real. Neat, huh?" she said, moving her hand to a leaf.

"Could have fooled me." Daxton said with a nod and a smile, relieved that at least someone was acting normal around him after yesterday's experience in Darkness.

"Where is B101?" he asked.

"This way. I am in that class as well," Halo said with a shy grin as she continued following a path of white flowers.

Walking into the brewtions classroom, Daxton took a seat and looked around. The room was divided into stations. There was an area with ingredients, an area to do the grinding, and a brewing station. The items to grind included a wide variety of beans, grains, and even pieces of various kinds of wood that filled glass vials. Bones covered the shelves near the brewing station. He thought those had to just be for show.

The grinding station had many short and tall grinders. Some looked like what Ms. Thelma used to grind sea salt or black pepper. Daxton looked around the station, studying the grinders. The most common was the one with small wooden boxes that opened for loading beans, grains, or stones, each with a handle for turning. Of course, this was all just what he guessed and what he'd seen from movies or read in books.

The last station was the brewing station, which had a multi-shaped metal infuser surrounded by many different teas and tiny teacups. The most interesting items were the brewing containers, each holding a filter at the top of a double glass container. The crushed beans or powder would go into the funnel. When the liquid was poured through the filter, the ground beans were then brewed, leaving liquid in the base of the glass container below.

He couldn't wait to start brewing. There, on the far side of the table, was a jar with an image of a beast and a growing plant on it.

I could even cure the infection that Brent and Tiffany still have.

"Welcome to brewtions. I am Madame Gia," she said, walking by Daxton's desk. Her orange hair looked even brighter up close, and her robe was made of huge elephant leaves. Daxton could see the dress underneath, which was made of beautiful flower petals. She looked like she came straight out of a forest.

"On your desk you have a starter brewtion kit, a stone mortar, and pestle, which you will use to grind different materials. It is important to always choose the correct ingredients and use them in the correct order. For example, you would never want to add sulfur to hot charcoal. To make a flameless fire, you wait until the charcoal is cool. Do it wrong and it will blow up in your face. In your bag, you will also find various types of water collected from all over, and of course beans. For now, you will use a grinder that is here, but others can be purchased from various vendors. Go ahead and look at your kits."

Daxton opened his brown box with the triangle earth symbol on it. Excitement overcame him as the aroma filled his nose. Once open, the box looked like a small lab with many tubes, vials, lots of different seeds, herbs, measuring spoons, an eyedropper, and a little candle. It's almost like science class at home.

Other than the candle, I guess.

"There is a vast number of brewtions one can make," Madame Gia said, fixing one of the lush, green leaves on her skirt. "The list is truly endless. But we must all start somewhere. Tonight we will make a Toad Wart brewtion. The key is to know what to use and in what order to add the beans or other items. You must also know if you have to add heat to the brew, or if you can simply mix the ingredients together. And do not worry if you do not yet have an array. Many brewtions, including this one, do not require elemental powers, only knowledge."

She stood in front of her own desk, which also had a mortar and pestle, a grinder, and many different ingredients. Daxton observed intently, wanting to know everything she was doing.

"Grinding your own beans is essential to consistency." She added some dark beans to the grinder. "These are black armo beans used for a hot beverage that gives you a bit of extra energy."

"Like coffee," Tiffany said excitedly.

Everyone turned and looked at her, confused.

We're never going to blend in here.

"Y-yes like coffee that our friends have in the Normal Lands," Madame Gia said, giving Tiffany a smile.

Daxton watched as Madame Gia grabbed a grinder and opened it, dropping in a bean, a flower petal, and some silver liquid from a vial before cranking the handle.

After a moment, a glowing silvery-blue liquid fell through the grinder's opening into a metal bowl. A rich aroma filled the room. While it may have processed something similar to coffee, it didn't smell like the coffee Ms. Thelma would make at home. This was sweet, almost sugary. Daxton took a deep breath, letting the aroma waft toward him.

She placed the metal bowl into a holder on the brewing station. "There are things you can add to it, like a crushed nightingale feather or red popper peppers, that will enhance your brewtion," she said, taking a sip from her tree mug.

Madame Gia moved back to her beans and ran her hands through some of them. "Extract is the purest form to work with. You are stripping the item, whether it be flowers, seeds, feathers, bark, metals, beans, stone, books, or whatever." She smiled at the hundreds of containers around her. "There are endless possibilities and combinations."

"Any questions?" Madame Gia asked, moving over to the grinding station.

"Yes, what could be extracted from a book?" asked Halo, thumbing through her brewtion book.

"Extra words, feeling, or emotion," Madame Gia said, running her fingers through blue beans that were in the shape of a crest.

"If you just set a bean in water, what will it do? Expand. Then, if you place them over heat, you can eat the bean. But if you grind the bean, plants, stone, or whatever you are using down to its most basic parts, you can make wonderful creations." Gia nodded, picking up a larger grinder before gathering a bowl with green smoke coming from it. "There are different grinders for different types of grinding, depending on what you want to extract from your item." She carefully selected a grinder that had a green, knotted handle with a leaf on it, and etchings of trees. Next she added some dark, metal bits and a portion of a snakeskin to the grinder. The room filled with the sweet smell of fresh pines. A thick, green substance oozed into a tiny vial with metal clasps for the top.

"Of course, while effective, not every brewtion will be pleasing to your senses."

Daxton and the children split up into pairs, pulled grinders from the wall, and gathered as many different types of items for grinding. Since Brent and Tiffany paired up, Daxton went with Halo, who seemed delighted with his picking of her. Each student took a turn at grinding and mixing their selections. Madame Gia would not let anyone use heat on their brewtions yet, but seemed delighted at the various outcomes of the brewtions.

A mix of aromas filled the room; not all great. Some were sweet, others rotten, but Gia smiled at every single student, so they had to be doing something right, even if it didn't smell like it.

"Imagine all the cool stuff we can do if we master this," Halo said, a huge smile on her face. "My family loves making brewtions. I can't wait to show them what I learned!"

The gongs rang out. Daxton quickly gathered his notebook and satchel. Brea popped her head out to lick his finger. "Soon," he mumbled. He wanted to ask Madame Gia more about bones, and turned back to ask, but she was already gone. Brent and Tiffany were already on their way out with their new friends. Stepping into the large hallway, he walked alone to his room where he released the eleagons and played with them for a bit before he felt the need to go outside. For the first time since being at Eldragor, Daxton paid heed to Madame Theresa's request and left the eleagons in his room.

Making his way outside, Daxton looked at all the students laughing and talking with friends. His mind went back to the orphanage, where it seemed like everyone had paired off, but he was left alone. Tiffany had Elizabeth. Brent had Isaac. Even Ms. Pat and Ms. Thelma had each other. Even in his own found family, he was the odd man out.

I shouldn't be surprised it happened here too. Even with this many people, I am alone.

In sadness, Daxton walked off towards the creek and was soon away from everyone else.

"Daxton," yelled Xander as he approached with Blair. "How dare you embarrass my sister in front of others? I will show you how to use a real array," he announced, flipping both palms out to illuminate two dark blue arrays. With a flick of his wrist, he pointed them at Daxton, who illuminated his array in defense.

Water from the creek moved in a wave that hit Daxton full on, knocking him to the ground. Caught unaware, as fear and anger invaded him, he writhed on the soaked ground, trying to get air into his water-filled lungs.

Blair laughed so hard that tears ran down her face. Xander flipped his wrist again, pointing at Daxton, causing the creek to wash over him again and again.

I can't breathe. I'm drowning.

Panic set in and Daxton flailed around in the water.

"XANDER LUXADOR," yelled a female voice from the nearby woods.

Xander turned to see a girl dressed in a dark green and brown tattered cloak that covered her brown and green pants and her shirt. Leaves, twigs, and dirt cover her face, hands, and clothing. In her right hand was a bow.

"If you don't leave that boy alone, I will make you. I am sick and tired of you picking on everyone weaker than you," she said, eyeing her target.

"Don't you dare talk to me, you waste of power," Xander ordered in a cruel tone as he maintained his illuminated arrays. "You know I am more powerful than you."

The girl glared at Xander. "Perhaps that is true most of the time, but you keep wasting your powers, while I do not." She pulled an arrow out from her quiver and attached it to her bow with a smile as her array illuminated.

Xander responded cautiously, "How dare you threaten me." He released the water of the creek, which flowed away from Daxton, and turned his attention to the girl, ready to attack.

Daxton lay there a moment coughing, feeling the burn in his lungs as he shuffled to all fours. He wanted to attack Xander, but was too weak.

"THAT'S enough!" Madame Theresa yelled at the entire scene, her array spinning as the wind pushed the water completely away. "Xander, you will not attack students." She said in an angry tone. "You will report back to the Aquaious Tower at this moment. I will talk to Elizabeth Pearl about this later."

Xander gave Daxton and the girl an evil look before moving away with Blair.

"Daxton," Madame Theresa asked in her authoritative tone, "Are you alright?"

Tiffany rushed to Daxton's side. "Yes, Daxton, are you alright? That boy is so mean. Just wait 'til I get strong enough. I will teach him a lesson or two."

"Yeah," Brent chimed in as he helped Daxton up.

Daxton coughed a bit, feeling his chest hurt. As he looked around, all eyes were upon him. It was strange how just over two months ago, Daxton never really had enemies, but he sure knew how to make them here in Eldragor. At this moment he figured he had three: Vulkan, Morpheus, and Xander.

"You will do no such thing," Madame Theresa ordered as she looked into Tiffany's eyes. She then gathered her wits while placing a hand on Daxton and patting his wet back. "Do try to stay out of the water," she said, checking him.

Daxton felt humiliated, but was thankful he could breathe again as he looked over at Athena, wondering what made her want to come to his rescue. He felt the soreness in his chest ease up a bit and gave her a soft smile to thank her for saving his life, while vowing to never go anywhere without his eleagons. With them, he was never alone.

CHAPTER 16 - PROPHECIES

It had been more than two weeks since Daxton's first day and he was beginning to get a handle on things. Luckily, the eleagons hadn't caused too much of a stir. Most of the students didn't seem to mind them, and, so far, he hadn't gotten in trouble for having them. The weeks had been filled with homework and learning everything he could. So far, he had not had any other altercations with Blair or Xander

Today, however, was Saturday and Daxton had been working on his array for hours when he decided to play a game of hide and seek with Brea.

Brea was not in her usual hiding places, so he decided to head outside to look for her when he saw Catherine coming from the far end of the hallway. He nodded, but she ignored him and walked the other way.

Rude!

He had not told anyone that she was also a Tanner and he didn't really know how to research the family, other than the obvious of going to the archives or asking questions about them. If he did that, would others begin to think he was planning on doing something like they did all those years ago? No, he needed a better plan; he needed to talk to someone specific, but who that someone was, he had no idea.

"Daxton!" Tiffany said, walking up behind him.

"What?" he said, putting his hand on the door that led outside to the courtyard.

"You're in trouble," Tiffany said, following him outside.

"We have been looking for you everywhere!" Brent said. "Theresa is mad."

"About what this time?" Daxton asked, taking a deep breath of fresh air. He smiled to see Brea flying around Theresa and trying to take a stick from her hand. Theresa also saw Daxton and headed straight for him.

This isn't going to be good.

"Daxton! I have told you to keep her in your satchel! Here I find her flying around like a bammble babble bee," Madame Theresa said.

"It's a game of hide and seek!" Daxton said.

"I don't care about your games!" Madame Theresa said, smacking the stick in her hand.

Brea growled.

Well, what's new?

THE ELEAGONS AND THE ELEMENTAL RIFT

Daxton snapped his fingers and Brea grabbed the stick with her tail before zooming into the satchel.

"I know Morpheus revealed your eleagons, which he should not have, but that doesn't mean that they can fly around whenever you feel like it! They must stay in your satchel, if not your room!" Madame Theresa ordered, her voice rising with every word.

"I will do my best!" Daxton said. His satchel bumped against him. He looked down. "They do have a mind of their own."

"Nevertheless, do as I say," said Madame Theresa, looking at Daxton's satchel.

"Yes, ma'am," Daxton said.

"Thank you! Now that I have all three of you together, I need to go and have your condition checked a bit better," her voice went low. "I must continue to be a sponsor for Brent and Tiffany until they are cured, which should have happened by now." She glanced at them, confusion clear on her face. "I feel if I knew more about you two, I could better prepare a brewtion." Her chin went up. "I am glad things are better for you, Daxton, but still, I would like to have things checked, just to be sure. The quill has never done that before, so we need to make sure you're okay. That you're all okay. With that being said," she paused. "We are going to fly to the far side of Pitch Black Forest."

Daxton started to protest because he had other plans this afternoon, but took a deep breath and he looked at Brent and Tiffany. He was glad Tiffany and Brent were still with him.

Theresa had placed a pair of spectacles around her neck, and it seemed that every time they were around she was scanning them.

"Excuse me?" Tiffany exclaimed, crossing her arms over her chest. "I hate heights."

In a flash, Theresa changed into her traveling trench coat and flipped her palm over to illuminate her array.

I hope I learn to do that so easily.

Small clouds began to form, and were soon large enough for a person to stand on. "Tiffany and Brent, you will not have control over yours," she said, walking over to the nicer one to stand.

"WHAT?" Tiffany asked loudly. "You expect me to ride a cloud?" Her head was shaking back and forth. "Um, it's made of air and water and…," she paused as she looked at Madame Theresa like she had lost her mind. "I'll fall right through."

"You will not," said Madame Theresa. "Oh, such nonsense."

"It's fine Tiffany," Brent said, standing on his cloud

"Oh! So you trust Mrs. Fancy Pants here to just not drop us or something? It would be a great way to solve her problem! I can see headlines! 'Kids fall to their death!'" Tiffany said, testing the white softness with her foot.

"I don't have time for this! Get on!"

"All right, fine!" Tiffany said, taking the cloud between her legs. "I'll ride it like a horse."

"You will do no such thing! Stand up," Madame Theresa said, blowing on a small black substance. "Oh, whatever," she relented as she saw Tiffany make no move to stand. "This is magnet powder, which will cause your clouds to follow mine."

Danton stood on his cloud, "Wait," he said. "Shouldn't you be controlling my cloud too?" he asked, pointing to his cloud.

"No, I have full faith you can do this."

Glad you do.

"Remember that there could be a vorous beast and it could hunt you again. The Rift has made it much more dangerous here. Do not wander off once we land," Madame Theresa said.

"Why are we going if it is so dangerous?" Tiffany asked, asked, tilting her head.

"We are going because the less people know you are infected the better," Madame Theresa said. "Are we ready?"

"Yes!" exclaimed Brent, pumping his fist in the air.

"It's just like you to want to fly to your death, Brent," Tiffany snapped, grabbing hold of the cloud tightly.

"You bet!" Daxton added, illuminating his dark purple array after several attempts.

He held steady as his array spun, changing from almost black and purple to a lavender as a gentle breeze pushed the cloud forward. The breeze increased, and he was soon zig-zagging across the sky entrance with a huge smile on his face.

Daxton felt alive, no longer wondering if he fit in or not, for he was flying a cloud in the sky. He loved the fresh air in his face and opened his mouth to bite a cloud. His laugh rang out, echoing in his ears. Riding clouds had come so naturally to him, he began to wonder if his parents had been surfers of the wind.

Could they do any tricks?

With a grin on his face as bright as the sun, Daxton turned his large cloud, owning the sky at that very moment. As birds flew by, he raced with them, laughing more. His pendant popped out from under his robe. While he moved, it bounced against his chest. Madame Theresa smiled, watching him race a white bird. "You remind me of me," Theresa said so quietly Daxton wasn't sure if he was supposed to hear. "So carefree."

With a twist of her hand, Madame Theresa's cloud shifted to the left and began to descend.

Daxton flipped his cloud with ease; his palms lowering the soft white puffiness to the tree line and then through the trees.

With an elegant stop and the formation of white stairs, Madame Theresa stepped down, placing her foot on the dark rooted earth. With a twist of her finger, her cloud swirled and disappeared. Brent and Tiffany's clouds came to rest on the ground and the two children stumbled off, looking up just in time to see Daxton fly in.

Daxton, who really didn't want to stop riding, hovered a few feet above the ground. He finally jumped off to join the others with a sensation of pride spreading over him as he flipped his wrist and twirled his fingers so that his cloud swirled and dissolved.

Pitch Forest was so dark that Daxton could barely see. The gnarled trees were hard to make out until he was close to them, but even the soft whispers of their branches rang loudly in his ears. Daxton's sense of smell was also sharpened; the foul stench of decomposing black leaves that lingered on the wind assaulted his nose. He was instinctively using the air to amplify sounds and smells. Although Daxton could barely make out a narrow path made of knotted roots, his ears detected an unknown sound from nearby that seemed to be getting closer. A green glow slowly approached, getting larger with every second. Daxton heard a woman singing a soft tune, and his pendant began to glow a faint green.

Out of the trees, Madame Gia appeared in a long dark green dress with a hooded cloak displaying a pattern of trees that helped her blend into her surroundings. Her green array was illuminated

THE ELEAGONS AND THE ELEMENTAL RIFT

and small vines moved around her. "Madame Theresa, it is good to see you. I am pleased you requested to meet here for an array foretelling. I do love spending my weekends out here so I can do my research," she said.

"Children, stay close," Theresa said, moving beside Gia. "I am really hoping to find something out about these three," she said in a failed whisper to Gia.

"I know," Gia said, walking forward.

From the center of the clearing, Madame Gia illuminated her dark green array and rolled a small cube away from herself like a die. The cube popped open, the sides lay flat, and a tree grew out.

Daxton's eyes widened as the branches sprouted into a laboratory. The roots grew a bookshelf and a wooden table, complete with teacups and sticks like trees. The leaves were replaced by drops of colorful elixirs. In the tree trunk was a brewtion station, and within it were many small limbs that acted as old hand-crank grinders. The last thing to grow was a massive oak podium with a very thick vine holding a thick leather book

Daxton moved about the tree as a green bubbit with branches for legs and arms pushed a cart full of beakers. Picking up a beaker, Daxton read the label, Vorous. The bubbit then moved over to a black drop of liquid and filled the beaker with it.

"What are these?" Daxton asked.

"Many things I use to make brewtions with," answered Gia curtly.

"And these?" Brent asked, pointing at a jar with black seeds.

"Shoo, get away from them!" Madame Gia said, grabbing the jar.

Brent took a step back, giving her a cockeyed look.

Daxton couldn't understand why she was acting so strange. Maybe she had drunk some bad tea.

"Now, where was I?" Madame Gia said, walking behind her desk. "Where are my glasses?" she asked, looking confused, trying to open the desk drawer. It wouldn't open. After a few moments, she illuminated her array and turned it to the door forcing it open.

Yeah, odd indeed.

"Lost the key," she said, putting a pair of spectacles on her nose. "Open," she ordered, trying to open the book. The vine smacked her hand. Madame Gia activated her array and mumbled under her breath. The vine crumpled and the book opened. She smiled half-heartedly. "Who's first?"

"First for what?" Brent asked.

"We are going to try to foretell if you will blossom any elements and if so try to determine how powerful your array might be." Madame Gia responded as she glanced over the children.

Daxton's nervousness took over.

What if Gia told everyone he was very weak and didn't deserve to be here? This is the only place I can find out about my family. And what about Brea and Blaze? They need to be around pure forms of their element. They'll never get that at home. I have to stay.

Madame Theresa looked confused and thought a moment before she spoke. "Brent and Tiffany don't have arrays. You know this already. You have been teaching them for weeks. They are imprinted with my array. Did you understand my obble?"

"Yes, yes. One was almost over the infection, but the other had the infection still coursing through her and you want to see why.

This is the first step. Just because they have no array does not mean they do not have some elemental power." Madame Gia finished and turned to Daxton. "For that one, you want to try to measure him. I understood the obble"

That one?

Without warning, Gia reached around behind Brent and swiftly plucked a hair from his head.

"Ouch!" Brent shouted, rubbing the back of his skull. "Why'd you do that?"

"I assumed you would not let me take your skin," she chuckled.

"S-skin?" Brent stuttered.

Madame Gia didn't answer, instead she placed her hand on the grinder. Then placed Brent's hair into a little opening in the trunk before closing it tight. The hair became a green and purple powder that fell into a copper bowl.

Daxton watched as Madame Gia picked up the copper bowl, dumping it into a teacup with element symbols. Pouring hot water over the powder, it sizzled as the air and earth symbols began to glow. Daxton noticed that Tiffany seemed to be upset by what Madame Gia had said about the infection.

The glow wasn't very bright, so Madame Gia picked the teacup to look at it. When she placed it back down, a tiny tiny tree grew.

"A very weak indication of a barely noticeable amount of earth and air, but not pure, with almost no trace of infection," Madame Gia said and then reached up to Tiffany to pull her hair, but Tiffany snapped out of her thoughts and dodged Gia's hand.

Tiffany's always been fast.

"No, no, no," Tiffany taunted. "Not going to happen."

Madame Gia shrugged and turned around, facing the vine by her chair. She then slyly stroked it lightly with her fingertips. "All right, young lady, have it your way."

As Tiffany smirked victoriously, the long base of the vine slithered across the floor and reached up behind Tiffany, snagging a strand of her blonde hair.

"That's not fair," Tiffany yelped, rubbing her skull.

Madame Gia repeated the same process to test Tiffany. This time, the hair changed colors from blonde to red then purple. As the hot water splashed into the cup, the air and fire symbols glowed faintly, but where the two triangles overlapped, it was black. Smoke fumed from the cup.

"So very weak," Madam Gia muttered. After a few moments, she blew on the smoke and watched as it latched onto the wall. "Air element, but not pure, and more than a trace of infection."

"How will I be able to protect myself with dirty air from one of those power-stealing monsters?" Tiffany asked.

Madame Gia turned to Theresa. "Have you tried adding sulfur to the wood and a touch of salt to the moon beans before you brew?" Madame Gia asked.

"Yes, I have tried everything."

"She was a Negment when you found her?"

"Yes! I ran the basic test. It was negative. Since the infection, it seems they have both evolved."

"Interesting," Madame Gia said, moving over to Daxton. "Yes, but the boy has just a small trace of infection," she said, pulling a piece of Daxton's hair. She repeated the steps for the third time.

Daxton watched as his hair was grounded in a multi-colored powder.

"Now, we know you have the element of air. This teacup will show us just how much we can expect," Madame Gia said, picking up the bowl and pouring it into a teacup that had levels on it.

Daxton watched as Madame Gia poured hot water into the teacup. It sizzled as a black tar bubbled up, exploding the cup.

What is that?

"Was that tar?" Madame Theresa asked.

"Yes, it can happen with the pure ones," Madame Gia said, offering a fake smile.

"The what?" asked Daxton, looking at the broken teacup.

"The pure ones," Madame Gia responded quickly.

"Thank you for your time, Madame Gia," Theresa said, almost just as quickly.

"Yes," Madame Gia said, moving her hand to a branch on the tree. The room retracted back into the cube. She placed it in her robe, and walked away.

When they landed back in Eldragor, Daxton's mind was still going over everything that happened with the foretelling. He was worried about his friends, and, as much as he enjoyed having them with him, he didn't want them to be hurt. When it came to his foretelling, and the way his hair turned to black goo and then exploded in that cup, Daxton wondered if he would eventually blow something or someone up with his air array.

Was that even possible?

As the others landed behind him, Daxton heard a scream in the distance. His heart raced and the air around him went cold. The screams got louder, and then they stopped; everything around him stopped and he realized he was on one knee.

"DAXTON!" Tiffany yelled, kneeling beside him.

"What was that?" Brent asked.

"I am not sure," Theresa said and hurried towards the source of the scream.

As they hurried around the corner, Raizy ran towards them, white as a ghost. "There's been an attack!" Raizy said, catching her breath.

"An attack?" Brent asked.

The roots on the ground were twice as long as normal. Moving back and forth like they were looking for something. As Madame Theresa approached, they quickly retracted. Out of the corner of his eye, Daxton saw Sengal staring at him, shaking his head in a look of disgust, or was it disappointment. Everything moved faster and his senses were sharper as he looked to see where Raizy had pointed to the garden. He moved closer, before Theresa got there, and he saw Catherine, motionless with her hands out in front of her as though she was using her array.

CHAPTER 17 - NIGHTMARES

Students were crying and screaming around Catherine, but it wasn't long before Theresa yelled at everyone to go to their rooms. No one wanted to, but it was clear how serious this was.

Once in his room, Daxton's mind was heavy. He wanted to help Catherine. He didn't know her that well, but if they were both Tanners they shared something, even if she didn't want them to, and now she might be gone.

No, I can't think like that. Theresa will save her, just like she saved Tiffany and Brent.

Daxton looked over at Brent who was on the floor playing with the eleagons.

Would he and Tiffany have turned to stone too? They looked so still.

He went to his desk to do the only thing he could think of as a distraction; homework. With Catherine on his mind, he pulled out his ink bottle, quill, and scroll from the center drawer. Daxton answered every question to the best of his ability, and then double-double checked everything. When it got darker, Blaze curled up on the desk letting his body give off heat and light so Daxton could continue to work.

With his homework done, he could try something new. Pulling out his book of brewtions, he reviewed the steps, placed the fidget in the mortar, and began to crush up a dead bug before adding the seed of a lily pad. Setting down the newly-ground mixture, he picked up the vial of toad water, dropped five beads of green liquid over the mixture, and watched it turn into a gooey, dark green solution. Daxton picked up the bowl, grabbed an empty vial, and let the solution drop into the vial.

Antiuum. Now I can help Brent and Tiffany! If they are not cured by the time we go home I can make this for them there.

Rain crashed against his window. It was so heavy that he couldn't see anything outside. The sky was black, and it seemed the rain matched. Thunder boomed, filling his ears. It sounded like it was in the room, but it had to be outside. After a quick, blinding lightning strike, he decided he couldn't continue his homework for the night.

Crawling into bed, Catherine's stone body played in Daxton's mind; the look of pain in her eyes.

Soon after he fell asleep, his palm opened suddenly and his array illuminated black. He tossed and turned with images in his head. A familiar voice grew louder as Morpheus came into view and then a man Daxton didn't recognize walked out into the eastern end of the main hallway,

"I know what you are saying, Morpheus, I just don't see how it would be possible," the man said.

"With the Eternal Tree on the brink of total destruction, I know what it means," Morpheus replied, illuminating his black array.

"How did you figure out it was me?" the man asked.

"I know your secrets. Go back to the hell that you came from!" Morpheus yelled.

The man stood. "Only if I take you with me!"

Morpheus attacked the man's body. His hollow face looked right at Daxton, whispering, "You must save her."

CHAPTER 18 – VULKAN

Daxton awoke with his heart pounding and his sheet wet with sweat. He took a deep breath, relieved that it was just a dream. Shaking off the awful feeling, he got out of bed. After preparing for the day, he moved over to his desk and saw that his book was open to a page with an emblem of two snakes that overlapped one another inside a triangle. Words then slowly appeared on the page: *Umbra Society*.

He grumbled to himself, knowing how temperamental the book was; there was no way to open the book until it wanted to. It would never make sense to him, especially because there were no other words.

Will I ever just get a straight answer from this place?

Brea took a deep breath and blew warm clouds around Daxton, as if she could sense his frustration. It was the closest thing to a hug he'd had in a long while. Daxton smiled, feeling the warmth of the clouds, and his mood relaxed a bit. "Thank you."

Blaze nuzzled against Daxton's giant cup of armo brew, keeping it piping hot for him. Daxton reached out, grabbed the mug, and took a long needed sip to warm his bones.

"At least you two never let me down," he said as each eleagon flew up to one of his shoulders.

Soon Daxton arrived at the large general area for breakfast, where the bubbits were busy making meals for the students. Large stacks of green pancakes, red fire bacon, and tons of flavored gelatin were piled high on triangle plates. Daxton's mouth watered while he watched a plate of purple eggs go by. A light purple bubbit quickly ran under his foot while holding out a purple triangle plate that had hashbrowns, purple eggs, and green pancakes on it.

This bubbit knew what Daxton liked to eat in the morning. Daxton was hungry, especially after last night's weird events. Another bubbit came around Brent and handed him a triangle plate, but it was green and filled with purple eggs and sausage.

"They sure know how to cook," Brent said, taking a whiff of the steam rising from his plate.

It wasn't as packed as usual, but there sat Tiffany with a half-eaten pink biscuit and tall tankard of pink frizz that was steaming from the top.

"Morning, sleepyheads," Tiffany said as they approached, before returning to the book she was reading.

"Morning, Tiffany," Daxton said, sitting down. "What are you reading?"

"A book on a variety of topics. I just finished reading about arrays," Tiffany said, flipping to a new chapter. "Do you think Catherine will be okay?" Daxton asked,

Tiffany answered without looking up. "Will she live? Yes? Able to use her array again? Doubtful. She will have memory problems and could imagine things. That makes it very difficult for a person to use their array because their head won't clear."

"How do you know?" Daxton asked.

"This book. It's a diary and talks all about it."

Daxton looked at the small diary that had two snakes inside a triangle on the cover. Something about it made his skin crawl. "Where did you get it?" he asked.

"There's a trunk under my bed that's full of books. Research and stuff. It looks like it's been there for years. Look at this," Tiffany said, dumping out her pink tote that was filled with articles, books, and scrolls.

"Tiffany, what is all this?" Daxton asked, looking at a piece of yellowed paper labeled, 1982: *CONGRATULATIONS LUXADOR on the Birth of a Baby Girl.*

"What's all this about?" Brent asked, raising his eyebrows.

Tiffany smoothed out the old paper. "I was lucky to find this. It talks about Annya. If it wasn't for that one picture hanging up by the Aeroious towers, no one would know that she ever existed. It's like someone wanted to erase her completely, and I am going to find out why. And that's not the only weird thing here." Tiffany placed the open book in front of him. Each page had four similar pictures of children with the Aeroious banner hanging above them. Below each was a caption with the date. Tiffany turned the page to find similar photos. The most recent was the picture taken this year before the Worthiness Ceremony.

Daxton and Brent looked at the pictures without responding.

"Don't you see it? Why do I have to explain everything? Look, they take one at the Worthiness Ceremony and then one at the end of the year," Tiffany said, nodding her head to prod them along.

"Yeah, so?" Daxton said, looking closer at the pictures.

Tiffany sneered, turned the page, and pointed at two pictures with the year 2010 on them. She held the book right in Daxton's face. "Do you see anything different?"

"Nope, just a bunch of kids in black and then in purple robes," Daxton said.

"Well, at least you can see that," Tiffany said, rolling her eyes.

Finally, he saw it. "This set of photos had eleven kids at the start of the year with only ten at the end." He flipped the pages forward and saw the same thing each time. There was one less student in the second photo of each year. Flipping back he saw that this was not the case before 2008.

Tiffany flipped through the pages. Dust was stirred as she did so. Eventually, Tiffany stopped at a sketched family tree that held basic information about each person. Tiffany read aloud, "Annya Luxador, born in 1982, is the daughter of Markus and Jessica Luxador. Ambassador of Eldragor from 2002 to 2006, Annya is famous for defeating Lord Dominus in 2008, stopping him from completing The Rift."

"Who's Lord Dominus?" Brent asked, tilting his head.

"I don't know," Daxton said. Hearing the name made a shiver crawl up his spine, inch by inch.

Closing the book, Tiffany picked up a folder labeled, *Acumens, Annya Luxador*. Inside were four certificates. Tiffany carefully picked up each of them and read, "Air 10, obtained in 2000. Fire 7, obtained in 2002. Earth 3, obtained in 2004. Water 3, obtained in 2005. It's no wonder," Tiffany said, placing each certificate back.

"No wonder what?" asked Daxton.

"That she died."

"What do you mean?"

"You can't have all four. And look at this," Tiffany said, grabbing another book. "This one mentions something called the Umbra Society."

Daxton's eyes went wide at this. He grabbed the book from her hands.

"It's apparently this weird society focusing on shadows instead of the other elements. There were a lot of members at one point. I don't know what happened to them, though," Tiffany continued.

Daxton read as she talked.

A society built from the ability to control shadows, the Umbra Society is dangerous.

"Daxton," said Brent, tapping his arm. Daxton looked up. "Let's go. We were going to go hang out with Ivan and Bjorn."

"Brent Thompson, can't you see that Daxton is looking at something. Be quiet for five minutes, could you?" Tiffany said, holding up her hand in front of his face showing her five fingers. "Look, it's not hard. You can count to five, can't you?" She lowered each finger one at a time to demonstrate counting to five.

"You always need to put your two cents in on everything," Brent retorted, slamming his hand down so hard that the fork he had been eating flipped up and smacked Tiffany right in the forehead.

"Oh!" Tiffany yelled, wiping her forehead.

"That will teach you!" Brent added.

Tiffany glared at him.

"Hush!" Daxton commanded firmly, grabbing Tiffany's book from the table and looking back and forth between his friends before flipping through the pages.

"She started it!" Brent protested.

"He started it!"

Daxton's heartbeat raced as he tried to find someone that looked like him. There was nothing. Flipping the pages in the book again, he came back to the list of names. He saw a few de Medici Drakes in the last few years, but no Tanners. How many of them was he potentially related to? How many were secretly Tanners? Tiffany and Brent's voices still rang in his ear.

As Tiffany stuck her tongue out at Brent, he picked up the fork from his green eggs and slung a chunk in her direction, hitting her hard on the nose.

Tiffany's mouth dropped and her eyes went big, and she picked up her fork. "It's on. Food fight!" she yelled.

Pulling air deep into his lungs, Daxton's voice boomed, "Stop!" before he returned to turning the book's pages. Unknown to him, a gust of wind flew from his spinning dark purple array. Everyone in the dining hall froze while all the eggs that Tiffany prepared to hurl at Brent fell harmlessly to the ground.

As everyone quickly regained the ability to move, they stared at Daxton, who didn't pay them any attention. He grabbed his things and headed out.

CHAPTER 19 - SKELETON KEY

What just happened? Did I do that? It couldn't be me, right? Sure Brent and Tiffany can be a little loud, but that wouldn't make me be able to just stop things, right? Maybe it wasn't even me. It could have been anyone. Yeah, anyone.

His mind was moving faster than it ever had before. As if knowing he needed a distraction, Brea and Blaze popped out of the satchel and flew around the hallway.

"Daxton, what's your eleagon doing?" Mr. Hopkins asked, walking towards him. Blaze flew just above his teacher's head.

"Blaze," Daxton said, looking at him. "He must like you."

"Well, I like him," Mr. Hopkins said, taking a cookie from his vest and giving it to him. Any time one of his teachers showed a liking to Brea or Blaze, Daxton felt like a weight was taken off of him. For all he heard about people not liking eleagons, the adults did not seem to mind.

"That's it, he must have smelled those cookies."

Blaze took the cookie with his paws and blew his fire breath on it, burning it immediately.

"He sure likes anything that's burnt," Daxton said, smiling

"Did you know that by heat, well the sun, we were able to tell time?"

"Yeah," Daxton nodded. "The sundial."

Brea flew over to Mr. Hopkins and sat on his head.

"All right, I got you one for you too," Mr. Hopkins said, giving her one.

Daxton smiled. He was glad that Mr. Hopkins liked Brea and Blaze. Ever since Blaze had found a pack of cookies in his clock door they had been like best friends. Watching Blaze eat the last of the chocolate chip cookie, he realized there was something that had been bothering him about the horology class. "I wanted to ask you something."

"Okay." Mr. Hopkins nodded.

"The key we got on the first day of your class, does it do anything?"

"Do anything?" Mr. Hopkins asked, inspecting Daxton through his spectacles.

"Yeah, does it open anything other than your classroom? I'm not really sure why you let me keep a key like that. You might need it."

Mr. Hopkins chuckled softly, and Daxton frowned, afraid he said something stupid.

"That key opens what needs to be open to you. A skeleton keys unlock doors only if what is behind a locked door pertains to the one holding the key."

More riddles. Great.

"Never fear, Daxton! Time is on your side," he said, checking his pocket watch. "Now if you'll excuse me, I need to go and get me some more cookies," he said, petting Blaze and then Brea.

His mind wandered to the key. Maybe he could find something it opened. He headed back to the old courtyard, passing through the archway to the Aero Tower, hoping to avoid all of the students after the food fight. He didn't want to talk about it; he didn't know how to talk about it. As he rubbed his hand over his face, Brea and Blaze flew just ahead of him.

They were always finding new things to explore. It was pretty impressive. They would find trees, new plants, or a hallway he'd never been down before. Walking outside, there were even new roots he had to step over.

The air around him changed instantly, becoming colder. A chill ran through him, then he saw her; Jessica. She was unmoving.

"Everyone back inside!" Ambassador Vulkan ordered as he approached. Several children took a step back, shocked by his booming voice. Daxton hadn't even noticed their approach.

"We have a problem, Vulkan!" Theresa shouted.

"I am fully aware of it, Theresa! This keeps happening and it's only going to get worse for your kind."

"You say 'my kind' one more time and I will show you what my kind can really do. Don't be so thick. This could have happened to anyone."

"Yes, it could have, but it didn't. The Aeroious students are being attacked and the only reason I can think of," he paused for a moment, looking at her.

"Then you admit you can no longer protect us!"

"How dare you!" Vulkan raged. "I'm doing everything I can to help these students and the tree. This is not the time to fight each other. We need to help her, now!"

Daxton stood there a moment as Theresa illuminated her array over Jessica's still body and lifted it up towards the castle.

"You better watch out or you could be next!" Sengal growled at Daxton as he walked by.

I could be next? What does that mean?

Daxton walked back inside; his mind heavier than it had been since arriving at Eldragor.

Something isn't right. What aren't they telling us?

CHAPTER 20 - VEIL OF DARKNESS

It had been two weeks since Jessica and Catherine were attacked. While both were now awake, their arrays were diminished. Their memories were almost just as bad. They would lose large chunks of time, showing up to most classes late. The two were sad and broken.

Classes had to continue, though. Daxton was advancing more and more towards becoming an elementor. He was figuring out more riddles and puzzles for Mr. Hopkins and he was doing well in Aerotion, able to make a cloud into a sword. Daxton was also advancing quickly in his array class, impressing Madame Theresa.

It was mid-morning on Saturday and Daxton was to meet Tiffany and Brent at the Elemental Archives right before lunch. It wasn't that far, but he could still get lost in this place after being here for six weeks.

When he reached the Tower of Knowledge, Daxton pushed open a heavy, oak door that led to a large, open room where there were many books hanging from trees. There was even a book that was a tree.

"Hey, Daxton," Tiffany said, sitting at a desk full of books.

"Have either of you felt your hand burn or anything?" Daxton asked, rubbing his hand over his left palm.

"No, nothing yet, but I'm hoping that something will happen soon," Brent said. "I don't know how long Theresa's imprint will last and I can't be re-imprinted. It's like a one-way ticket."

"Well, that's just great, so either something happens, or we can never return," Tiffany exclaimed, looking up and stopping a bubbit walking by. "Do you have any books about The Rift?"

The little bubbit looked at Tiffany, and then took its arms and legs inside its body and rolled over to and up the stone stairs. It moved quickly until it stopped on the fourth level of shelves. The green bubbit bounced from one bookcase to another until it landed on a large cloud that held just one book. The bubbit pushed it from the cloud and it landed right in front of Tiffany.

Nice shot!

"Thank you," Tiffany said, picking up the large leather-bound book with 'Veil of Darkness' written on it in black lettering. She flipped the book open, and dust flew from inside. There she studied an article and read out loud, "The Veil of Darkness. Will we ever see the end? It's getting more hopeless as the days go on. The storms never cease, and the quakes last for hours. Maybe the Normal Lands could give us a chance for peace?"

Daxton listened to Tiffany as she read. The book was filled with newspaper clippings. Only a few clippings had to do with the Rift or the Master of Darkness, though. She went on to read,

"Did Annya Luxador know that once she overcame him, that his veil would remain in Eldragor, or that she just paused the Rift. Was this her plan to ruin us? Even though he is banished from Eldragor, his essence remains. Will the island continue to destabilize? We know for sure our lands will no longer be filled with the beauty it once was. It will now be a haven for the evil that it contains. Kur plants will rise, ghouls will stalk us, and even the winds and rains will be against us. Yes! Yes! I ask you, will it ever end? No, for it will be only a matter of time before he returns to finish what he started. If he is not already among us." Looking up from the clipping, Tiffany asked, "What does it mean to continue to destabilize?" She read the lines again and began to panic. "If this means that it will never go away, then what am I going to do about this infection? I can't live like this forever."

"Tiffany, if this was the case, don't you think it would have happened by now?" Brent asked.

"How do you know it's not happening right as we speak," Tiffany replied.

"Because if it was, we would know," Brent said, putting his hand on her shoulder.

"Would we? Daxton, what are we going to do? I don't want to destabilize."

Daxton sat there a moment, looking at them. "When was this written?"

Tiffany looked. "In 2008."

Daxton nodded. "Well, Eldragor is still here, so the lands are not gone yet, and well, if a Rift did come," he paused. "Vulkan would not want to wipe everyone out. You'll be okay."

"What if he just wants to wipe out the weak?" Tiffany asked, slamming the book. "This stupid book doesn't say anything about him! Who he was, what he did, or where he came from, just Veil of Darkness!" she said, her hands going up in the air.

"It'll be okay. We won't let anything happen to you. Let's go eat."

She nodded, looking less panicked, but still a little dejected.

After dinner, everyone moved out into the courtyard holding bags of colorful popcorn as obbles floating around the castle would periodically pop and say, "Vendors of Spixie Caravan will be here next weekend! Have your shopping list ready.

"What is the Spixie Caravan? I keep hearing about it," Brent asked.

"It's a caravan to which elementors can transport through mirrors," responded Halo as she walked by. Stopping, she turned and faced Daxton. "Its merchants have odd items and hard to find ingredients, but I like the popcorn kernels. They don't come that often so when we get to go, it's awesome. Food, drinks, animals, it has anything and everything,"

"What is a spixie?" Daxton asked.

"Spixies are born from Elementor's tears. Kinda like an emotion so powerful it forms into a ball of energy and that energy forms into a familiar; someone that the Elementor can rely on."

"Do all elementors have them?"

THE ELEAGONS AND THE ELEMENTAL RIFT

"Oh no, only a handful of elementors have ever had eleagons. Spixies are sorta like eleagons. A spixie is bound to its ward."

Daxton thought about that a moment as he looked up at Brea and Blaze. Was he keeping them from something great or did they choose to be with him?

"What do they look like?" Tiffany asked.

"Well, like little, tiny people with wings," Halo replied.

"Oh, you mean like a fairy?" Tiffany asked.

"I don't know what a fairy is," Halo said.

"Well, fairies are tiny and have wings and can do stuff," Tiffany said.

Halo shrugged her shoulders. "That must be a Normal Lands thing. Spixies are small and very temperamental and don't answer to anyone but their ward," Halo said, looking at Tiffany. "Anyway, we all go to Six Elixirs to get drinks after we're done shopping. You should come with me. But I'm off to finish my project before the weekend," Halo said, walking away.

"Daxton, are you thinking what I'm thinking?" Tiffany asked, looking at him.

"Tiffany, we are never thinking the same thing," Daxton said.

"Well, what if we can find an eleagon there! I would be the first Negment to have one!" she said, forgetting all about her sadness from earlier in the day.

"Tiffany, we talked about this weeks ago. I don't know if you looking for an eleagon is a good idea."

"Why?"

"Well, as you know they are banned, and I just don't think it's a good idea."

"You have two." She frowned.

"Yeah, and that's what I am trying to tell you. It's dangerous."

"Are you trying to tell me what to do, Daxton?"

"No, I'm just saying I don't think you should look for one, but let one come to you. If it's meant to be, it will be. I didn't look for Brea or Blaze. They found me."

"Well sometimes, things need a little push."

Yeah, a push off the deep end.

Daxton needed to think by himself.

What's she going to do? Walk up to every spixie and ask for an eleagon?

Taking a deep breath, he watched as Brea and Blaze hovered close, making their way to the far corner of the courtyard. It just didn't make sense to him why Tiffany wanted an Elegaon; she didn't have an array and he was sure that Madame Theresa was going to cure her. But what if she found one while she was infected? Would it become infected too? But if nobody else has one, then there was no way she would get one.

Rounding the corner, he heard voices. Vulkan and Morpheus were having a heated conversation. Daxton needed to know what about. He quickly moved over to the remains of a pillar and hid behind it, trying to overhear their conversation.

"What are you doing?" asked Brent, walking up from behind.

"Shh."

"About the Cain brewtion, have you found a way to make it work without the side effects?" Vulkan asked in a serious voice.

"No," Morpheus replied. "The brewtion recipe that Master Cain provided was useless."

"Then things are destabilizing faster than we expected and no one will be able to stop The Rift this time."

The Rift! I knew they were up to something!

Vulkan and Morpheus moved further away, so Daxton could no longer hear them. Daxton saw Morpheus go one way and Vulkan the other. Blaze moved to Daxton's shoulder as Brea flew ahead following Morpheus.

"The Rift? Daxton, did I hear him right?" asked Brent.

"Yeah, it sounded like he is going to try and start one or finish what the Master of Darkness couldn't."

"That could explain all the storms lately. Do you really think they would do that though?"

"I'm not sure of anything when it comes to those two."

Daxton and Brent followed carefully behind, finding an old passageway from the North Tower. Morpheus was gone, though; they lost him. Frustrated, Daxton stamped his foot on a stone, which began to move. The stone gave way to stone steps. Daxton and Brent glanced at each other before following the steps down to a passageway..

The passageway led to an opening, and Daxton crept into a room and saw a cauldron over a fire with a dark brewtion simmering in it. The smell was awful; worse than the rotten eggs they had found at the orphanage a year after they were hidden. On a shelf were several beakers, each filled with a different color liquid. The beakers were labeled with the new Aerious students' names. A chart to the side had high/low markings that corresponded to each beaker. A black beaker with Tiffany's name on it had the highest markings.

"I bet," Daxton said, pressing his finger to Tiffany's name, "this is how they see who's weak."

Brea moved over to a cup of rainbow freeze. She dove in the small cup, knocking it over.

"Brea!" fussed Daxton.

"Do you think Morpheus would use a green quill feather?" Brent asked.

"No."

"Or drink green wart slime?"

"Nope," Daxton said, shaking his head.

"Then I don't think this is his study," Brent said slowly.

"Then whose is it?" Daxton needed answers. He moved to the shelf and found an empty vial of sulfur and darkness. He then went to the desk and saw an old brewtion book that had to be older than the castle itself. The pages were fragile, and he feared it would crumble to dust if he touched it. Next to it was an award that read, Best Brewtion.

As Daxton and Brent moved quietly down a dark hallway, they found a door that was open. There on the floor was a lilac flower. Picking the dainty purple flower up, Daxton studied it for a moment.

What is this flower doing here?

CHAPTER 21 - VOROUS BEAST

"The light! The light!" Brent yelled, pulling the cloud blanket over his head to shield his eyes. He started making light hissing sounds, almost like he was melting.

"The what?" Daxton asked in a panic.

Brea, who had made a nest on top of Daxton's head in the middle of the night, flew backward as Daxton sprang from his bed.

"Brent, it's just the morning."

Brea caught herself by arching her wings and then flew around to Daxton and looked at him. Daxton reached up and petted her head.

"Well, I would like it to stop being morning so I can go back to sleep. You'd think in a place where everything was made of clouds, they'd have better curtains."

Daxton chuckled as his friend sat up in bed.

"Do you really think Morpheus and Vulkan want to start another Rift?" Daxton asked, a sudden seriousness to his voice.

"Yeah, that's what it sounded like," Brent said, pulling the covers off his head. "But why?"

"So they would be in total power."

"How can we be sure?"

"I don't know, but I bet you that chart and this flower have something to do with it."

When Daxton sat down at breakfast, Brea and Blaze immediately jumped out of the satchel, bothering the bubbits.

"Brea! Blaze! Behave," Daxton said, a sigh escaping his lips.

Luckily, most of the students who had seen them didn't mind the eleagons. Amon smiled as Brea flew over his head. Bjorn scratched Blaze's ear as he got close to the boy. Yes, he was lucky when it came to the students.

It was the adults he had to worry about; mainly Morpheus and Vulkan. Morpheus had an odd reaction when he discovered the eleagons all those weeks ago, seeming disappointed that they were attached to Daxton. In the classes that followed, Daxton couldn't help but notice his teacher staring at his bag. Vulkan had not said anything since the ceremony, and Daxton was grateful for that. If they got their hands on Brea and Blaze…, he didn't even want to think about it. He didn't have much time to think anyway. It was time for class.

Daxton learned the hard way that timing was crucial. Ever since his first brewtion didn't turn out right and he had to pour it out, Daxton had paid extra attention in Brewtions. He watched Madame Gia carefully, noting how she diced and chopped the ingredients. He took detailed notes, wanting everything to be perfect. Daxton quickly caught on and when he made mistakes he was able to correct them.

After today's class, Daxton made a quick trip to the library to grab as many books as he could on plants To help him prepare for his brewtions assignment, which was to grow a plant and then use it in a brewtion.

He grabbed several books on various types of plants and hauled them out of the library quickly. As he ran out of the library, he saw Madame Gia heading away from her class.

"Madame Gia," he called.

She ignored him. Daxton said her name louder. She hesitated, but eventually turned around. "What?" she snapped.

She must be having a bad day. This isn't like her. Other than her temperament, her wardrobe was bizarre too. Instead of her usual green outfit filled with twigs and flowers, she was in a simple black dress. Was she wearing that during class? I was too busy with notes to see.

"What is the best plant to experiment on," Daxton asked quietly, not wanting to get on her bad side.

"What for?"

"The assignment?"

"What assignment?"

"The one you gave us. Don't you remember? We each have to grow our own plant and then use it to create a special brewtion. You said it would help us students understand plants, our abilities, and ourselves better. I have not decided what plant to use."

"Right, of course. Mistletoe is a great plant, especially for your love life. There are some vines in my office. Why don't you come get them and see what you can make with them?"

"Really? I thought we have to grow them." Daxton responded.

"Oh, don't worry about that. You don't have time or the proper trees to grow mistletoe. Come now," Madame Gia answered with a smirk and walked slowly to her office, looking at each door she passed before continuing on. It was like she forgot where her office was.

It must be a really bad day.

Once they reached her class, she gave him a strand of mistletoe with its white berries. "Have fun," she said.

It didn't seem right, but she was the teacher and knew what she was talking about. He grabbed the mistletoe. "Thank you," he said before hurrying to his room.

Once there, he placed the mistletoe on his desk. Now that he did not have to spend time getting the plant to grow, he had plenty of free time, so Daxton went outside.

Once outside in the fresh air, he flipped his right palm over to illuminate his array. The purple circles spun while gathering the air around him until it formed a white fluffy cloud. With a grin, he jumped onto it. Slowly, it moved. Feeling the cloud firm under his feet, he moved his palm around until he got the hang of directing the cloud. With a smooth movement of his hand, the cloud took off.

The day was suddenly perfect; no stress, no worries, just him and his eleagons flying. The feeling of freedom rushed through his veins as he saw nothing except the top of tree branches. He did not worry that he was not supposed to be away from the castle grounds as he enjoyed the warmth of the sun on his face and the rushing air all around.

As the trees became darker and more ominous, Daxton realized just how far from the castle he was, and suddenly the howl of the wind grabbed Daxton's attention. Something was different. It grew louder and seemed to be at a different pitch than it had been. Daxton stopped his cloud. He knew this sound; he had heard it before. Slowly he hovered over the edge of Pitch Forest with Brea and Blaze flying nearby.

The sound of a horrible scream filled the air and all three were shocked. Daxton's heart skipped a beat as his blue eyes darted to a figure running out of the forest. Daxton flew toward the girl with blonde hair running.

What does she think she is doing out here alone?

"HELP! HELP! It's chasing me!" the girl yelled. The voice sounded familiar.

Something dark loomed behind her.

"I'm here!" he shouted while Brea made Daxton's cloud larger and Blaze blasted fire at the shadow creature, causing it to veer off course. Daxton swooped down to the girl, put his arm around her, and hoisted her onto his now larger cloud.

"Tiffany!" he blurted.

"Daxton," Tiffany fussed. "A vorous beast is chasing me. Help me! Hurry!"

Daxton quickly flew them up and away toward the safety of Eldragor. Glancing back, Daxton saw no sign of any creature in pursuit of the cloud. The two children remained quiet during the flight back.

"What made you go into the forest?" Daxton asked as they approached the courtyard.

Once on the ground, Daxton helped his friend off the cloud. Tiffany was as white as a ghost. She stood there, breathless, trying to regain her composure. It took a minute, but soon her complexion returned to normal and she calmed slightly.

"You almost got me killed! Where were you anyway?"

"What?" Daxton asked in confusion.

Tiffany pulled a note from her robe and shoved it in his hand. "Next time you ask me to meet you, you better be there!" she said, storming off.

Brea and Blaze zipped into Daxton's satchel.

Now what?

From the shadows came a form. Daxton knew it was Vulkan by his giant strides. He gulped as the man got closer.

"Daxton! Where is Tiffany! Is she all right?" he asked, beads of sweat dripping from his forehead. Something about him didn't seem right, but Daxton couldn't figure out what. He wondered if it was just the rage that made him a little off.

"Sir?" Daxton asked, curling the note up in his hand.

How did he know it was Tiffany I rescued?

"Tiffany!" Vulkan said. "I heard her scream."

"She was in danger," Daxton responded. "A Vorous Beast almost got her and me at the edge of the forrest!"

Vulkan gulped and pulled his cloak up higher around his neck. "I see. I will have to find a way to stop the beast."

Daxton nodded and walked away, confused. He knew Ambassador Vulkan was a weird guy and all, but that conversation was odd. Vulkan had never cared about Tiffany. Why did he care now? And how did he hear her screams from so far away? With that thought, Daxton uncurled his hand and read the note:

Tiffany,

I need your help. Please meet me in the forest where we did the foretelling. It's really important. Come alone.

-Daxton

He didn't write this. Someone had lured Tiffany out into the forest.

But why?

CHAPTER 22 - CONGRATULATIONS

By the next day, everyone learned he had outrun a vorous beast on a cloud and there was no word if the beast had been caught or not. Catherine and Jessica were still out of it. Dr. Sneererse was working hard to cure them. Daxton still had his guard up around Morpheus and followed him when he could. He watched the clock in brewtions, waiting for class to end. According to his notes, Morpheus would be in the courtyard.

The gongs rang and Daxton hurried straight to the courtyard. There Morpheus was talking to Vulkan under a tree, shadows obscuring most of their faces. Daxton tried to get closer, but he didn't want them to hear his breathing. It didn't matter. It wasn't two seconds before they exchanged words and walked away from one another. He missed everything.

Daxton nodded at Ivan, Bjorn, Amon, and Nicholas, who had just entered the courtyard. There was laughter coming by the fountain where Halo, Zoey, Tiffany, and Valerie were gathered.

"Halo, do you know what seeds you are going to use for your 'grow me' project?" Tiffany asked.

"Well, the perfect pink performances are in and I thought I could use them? What about you?"

"The fire cherry," Tiffany said with a smile on her face.

"Come on, let's go to the garden."

Daxton heard them and knew he didn't need to get a seed,

But he wanted to try and talk to Tiffany about the note she thought he wrote. Daxton followed close behind the group. Halo waved at him and he nodded back.

They made their way from under the arched walkway to the path leading to a small hut where Sengal lived. It was next to the garden and had a large greenhouse. It was the perfect place for finding seeds.

There they saw large pumpkins, squash, and melons being picked by the earth bubbits and lots of rows of new sprouts. Seeds of every kind filled numerous shelves. Senegal was not around, but there on his workbench lay a map with a colorful tree in the center and several black seeds. Iris was already there.

"Hey, Iris," Tiffany said, lifting her hand to wave.

"Hey, Tiffany," Iris said, holding a green pumpkin. "I don't know what seed you're picking, but be careful picking up a pumpkin because the thorns will prick you." She held out her palm, a small trickle of blood flowing.

"Are you hurt?" asked Tiffany in concern.

"No, not really," Iris said reaching for a cloth to wrap her hand.

Brea was busy eating a large strawberry, and Blaze was on the ground growling at roots that moved.

Daxton looked at all of the plants and seeds, glad he no longer had to pick one.

"How long are you all staying out here?" he asked Iris, trying to find a way to talk to Tiffany.

"Not too much longer. The Spixie Caravan is tonight and Tiffany and I need to go get ready."

Daxton had completely forgotten that it was tonight.

"That's right," Tiffany agreed, bending over a small pumpkin to reach for a fire cherry flower. "This one will do perfectly. I'll just need to get some seeds out of it." She picked out two seeds and several pumpkin roots reached up and scratched her hand, shrinking back immediately when the blood appeared. "Ouch! That gardener really needs to get rid of these roots."

Daxton tried to approach Tiffany, but she hurried out to take care of her now bleeding hand. The other two girls gathered what they needed and quickly followed.

Missing his chance, Daxton decided to go work on his brewtion before the caravan.

Daxton slowly wandered to his room, deep in thought about how to explain the note, and how to convince Tiffany it was not him. Once in his room, he went to his desk and pulled out his brewtion kit. Slowly he opened the box, looking at all the vials and his mortar and pestle. He selected some ingredients and tossed them into the mortar. Daxton then crushed the ingredients with the pestle and added a drop of water. The mixture turned to a milky white solution as he continued to work it. Unsure of what it would do, Daxton took a swig.

Hmmm nothing.

Suddenly a severe abdominal pain struck him and he fell to the floor. Grasping his stomach, Daxton rolled around until he lost consciousness.

Surrounded in darkness, he saw Ambassador Vulkan making notes in his chambers. Vulkan grumbled about something and ripped up the scroll he was writing on. The image became blurry and Daxton was now in the courtyard. When he looked up, his eyes widened at the sight of the Eternal Tree. He reached out his hand and felt a thorn prick against his finger. A drop of his blood landed in a vial Morpheus held.

Daxton snapped awake. An immense pain made his finger throb. Looking down, dried blood coated the tip of his finger.

How is that possible?

CHAPTER 23 - SPIXIE CARAVAN

Daxton continued to stare at his bloody finger, spooked. He was supposed to visualize Brea and Blaze before he slept and he had not, leaving no protective barrier during his nap; no protection, and someone was able to take something out from his dream. He couldn't let this happen again.

Why did the brewtion make me sick?

Needing to learn more about what happened, he went to his satchel and pulled out the book. Two pairs of eyes blinked up at him.

Good to see you.

Opening the book, he smiled when he saw it was the section on eleagons. His smile quickly turned to a frown as the book confirmed what others had told him: eleagons needed elemental energy to grow, evolve, and survive. If they didn't get this kind of energy, they would die. The book closed on him and would not open, refusing to let him learn about what happened in his dream.

Thanks for not giving me any useful information.

Frustrated, he made his way downstairs.

Everyone was in the center of the Sky Dome, talking and getting ready for their trip to the Spixie Caravan. He was so excited to actually be going there. He'd been hearing about it for weeks, and he wouldn't let his dream ruin this moment.

"You reckon we will get to see any spixies?" Bjorn asked, shifting his weight.

"Probably," Amon answered. "They are really neat."

"I also want to go to Six Elixirs," Bjorn said, counting his coins. "They have the best drinks."

Daxton listened as he moved to stand by Zeke.

"You'll spend all your coins there and then I will have to buy your drink like that time my parents took us," Bjorn added.

"Yeah, what are friends for?" Amon said with a smile.

"Not to pick up your tab all the time," Bjorn responded, putting his coins away.

"How are we going to get there?" Brent whispered to Tiffany.

"It's nice of you to ask, Brent," Madame Theresa answered as she entered the room, walking toward the large mirror on the south wall. "Everyone knows that mirrors are really portals to the unknown. Any elementor that wants to visit the Caravan needs only to write the proper symbol on a mirror. When it glows, it means that the vendors are coming in one week." She moved her finger over the mirror to show a previously hidden glowing symbol of two connecting wings, similar to a sideways figure eight. "The Spixie Caravan will be set up like a flea market. There will be a large selection of vendors selling or trading their goods. They move to a different location each month, basing their movements on the moon, but very few people understand. Different colors signify how long until it opens." She pulled out a pouch of black powder labeled 'Daizy Magnets' and tossed some on everyone.

Daxton sneezed and felt the powder clinging to his robes. As each particle touched his skin, it gave him a tingle of energy that seeped into the very core of his bones.

"This powder acts like a magnet and will follow my obble so no one gets lost," Madame Theresa explained. "Now, everyone must do exactly what I do."

She pulled out her vial and blew an obble, which grew bigger and bigger and bigger. Next she blew two smaller obbles for Brent and Tiffany. Finally, she stepped into it and nodded for the others to do likewise. The children used the obble vials they received in class. Amon and Nicholas had no problem. Raizy's had a place inside for her to sit and Brent's only covered up to his head, so he had to squat to fit. Several older students that Daxton had not met quickly blew theirs and fit inside perfectly. Daxton was the last to get his to work. He blew it up and very carefully stuck his foot inside. Touching the bottom of the obble with his foot, it felt like it was ready to take flight. He climbed in and squatted nervously inside what felt like a cocoon. The obbles suddenly lined up one after the other.

Daxton looked around, making sure Madame Theresa didn't notice that he brought his eleagons with him. She spoke through his obble as though it had speakers on both sides of his head. It sounded so close that it startled him.

"Just waiting for the right time," Madame Theresa explained.

Brea and Blaze poked their heads out of the satchel, looking around at all the excitement. Brea blew Blaze's mane and tried to scamper away from the satchel. Daxton pushed their heads back in. "Behave," he said in a low voice. "I don't want you two getting lost."

The chimes of the grandfather clock struck nine. The sound rang out throughout the great dome and on the third chime, the mirror turned black.

"They are open!" Madame Theresa said excitedly. "Okay. One, two, three, Spixie Caravan if you please." The obbles were sucked into the mirror one by one, like cars on a train.

Air swirled around inside the obble, becoming a glowing mist that pulsed on Daxton's skin, giving him a glowing appearance. It was difficult to tell where his skin ended and the air began. Beams of light permeated his very core. He became one with the light, and everything, including the other students, was a blur as they sped through the unknown darkness. Daxton felt like he was going to be sick. A beam of light appeared ahead. As it grew, Daxton made out what looked like a blurry village. Everything came quickly into focus and he realized he was heading straight for the pavement.

"AHHH!" Daxton screamed as the obble came to a sudden stop, cushioning his fall to the ground as it popped. He landed on top of other children and regained his composure as he watched the others fall.

"That was awesome!" Brent shouted, hopping up with a huge grin.

"Do not wander off alone, and be back in an hour," Madame Theresa said, handing them each twelve blue coins. "There is a section of caravans that is off-limits because you are too young, so do not go there. Furthermore, it is dangerous, and unless you want to get robbed, stay away from that area." She eyed each of the children warily. One of the vendors wandered up to Madame Theresa to show her different types of feathers. "If you need anything, I will be in the Elegant Plume," she said, turning to leave.

Daxton took in the smell of rich apricots as his eyes scanned a variety of lamp posts, covered wagons, makeshift tents, and all sorts of floating objects. None of the merchants had permanent shops, but stood in front of wagons and tents. It reminded Daxton of stories he heard as a child about gypsies who would move around from city to city in wagons setting up markets.

"Where to first?" Daxton asked, hoping Tiffany would stay with him and Brent so he could talk to her.

"Come with us," said Halo, grabbing Tiffany's hand.

"Don't leave without me!" Tiffany called out to the boys.

Daxton and Brent headed off in a direction where they saw five little girls with long colorful skirts and black braided hair chasing a pink spixie. There were various wagons and tents where elementors shopped for different items such as vials filled with eyeballs, freezing bombs, disappearing beans, or liquid fire. There was an earth merchant dancing in a long green gown with a top made from huge leaves. Another vendor shouted that she was giving away free samples of Acorn Fizz, a beverage she claimed was guaranteed to improve one's physical and mental attributes.

"Get it now! It will make you smarter, taller, and, yes, my dear, even beautiful!" the woman's voice called out.

Upon walking farther on the dirt path, the two boys spied an old two-story, rugged wagon with red lettering spelling 'Epic Elnimals.' Cages full of animals were piled up outside as well as inside.

"You interested in a Felis Cat?" a short man inquired, holding a pipe.

"A what?" Brent asked, jumping back.

"A Felis Cat," the man repeated, squinting his one good eye.

"No," Daxton said, moving over to look at the cage with the words 'Felis Cat.' Its fur was short and made from fire. "That cat looks like he's on fire."

"Nah," the old man said, opening the cage. "It's just his fur," he informed as he petted him. "The more you pet him, the hotter his fur flames, but it's not really fire."

"Neat," Brent said, petting the little beast. "Kind of like Blaze."

"No," Daxton stated in a low voice, "Blaze gets hot and can set things on fire."

"You have a beast that can set things on fire?" the man asked, putting the cat back.

"No," Daxton said, shaking his head as he held his satchel close to him and moved over to look at another beast in a cage. He was startled that the man had overheard him.

Does he know we were talking about an eleagon? Does he want it?

Wanting to change the subject quickly, Daxton looked around the area and saw a soft blue owl perched on a stand.

"What about this blue owl here?" Daxton asked.

"Ah! The Sphinx Ice Owl," he said, opening the cage. "I can give you this one for a good price. It should be able to live in the Normal Lands." His hand slowly petted the light blue owl that was now perched on his arm.

What does that mean? 'Should be able' to live there? And how does he know I'll be going back to the Normal Lands?

"I was just curious what it was," Daxton said, looking around and reading the names on the cages.

"Be careful of the Lobos; it will bite."

Daxton jumped back, seeing a wolf with grass for fur.

"Do you have any bigger creatures?" Brent asked.

"Like?"

"A water horse?" Brent suggested.

"Those things are hard to keep and are almost as rare as unicorns," the man answered.

Both boys looked disappointed. Tiffany would have loved to see a water horse.

"I do have a seahorse," the man said as he pointed at a small bowl of water with a single seahorse. "I had to travel to the Normal Lands to get it. Very rare."

"No thanks," Daxton said.

Rare? They have them for sale in the fish section of the big store in town back home.

"Daxton, don't look, but there's a female spixie that keeps looking at me," Brent whispered. "We should go talk to her."

"Okay. We have time. I can watch you get turned down by a spixie," Daxton said with a laugh.

The two boys made their way toward the purple spixie without being too obvious, but she realized they were coming to her and she flew away.

They hurried down the alleyway a bit, passing a big orange and green caravan. Daxton lost the spixie from his view. This vendor section had much less activity, though. Daxton felt like someone was watching him. As they walked, a strong, unpleasant odor wafted toward them. The yellow beams of the glowing lamps cast an eerie glow on a sign warning that only spixies and advanced elementors were allowed beyond.

Daxton and Brent continued, but the spixie was nowhere to be seen. A spooky noise echoed through the small area. The boys found words scrawled on the side of a black caravan, which was overgrown with moss and large cobwebs that framed the dark, stained windows. The beaten-up sign read, 'Tinctures 'n Tonics.'

"Well, we came this far, we might as well see what is inside," said Daxton nervously.

Brent started to answer, but jumped as a black spider dropped on his head. He let out a little yelp. Curling his hands and trying hard not to scream, Brent bolted from the side of the caravan and ran up the black broken steps, shaking his head. "Get it off me! Get it off me!" he pleaded, fleeing into the safety of the spooky caravan.

Brent was usually interested in any creature, but spiders were his weakness.

Daxton could not help but laugh. "It's off," he said, following Brent inside. The inside was larger than what it looked like on the outside. There were many weird things that reminded Daxton of a voodoo shop he once read about in a story. Scattered around were dolls, skulls, dream catchers, snake skins, beads, oversized cotton balls, and many other oddities placed on shelves. Further back were glass cases with brewtions in front with a wide variety of ingredients. On one of the cases was an old register made of different metal parts and behind it, a cabinet labeled 'The Darkest of Elements.'

Brent rang a bell that sat on some cases.

DING!

"Who's there?" called an old man from the rear. The boys were startled, but Brent moved toward the voice. A hunched over man stepped into the room from a doorway to another room. He had a fringe of gray-white hair around his balding, mottled scalp and a huge mole on his chin. His elderly face was heavily lined with wrinkles and a long, crooked nose poked out above a mouth lacking several teeth. The man wore a worn-out overcoat and seemed not to be able to stand up straight. Each laborious movement he made using his cane was joined by the creaking of old bones.

"What are you two doing on this side of the park? You're too young to be over here," the man said as he squinted, looking the boys up and down.

"Oh. The sign didn't say anything about age. We're advanced," Daxton answered while Brent checked his hair for more spiders.

"Well, not my business to care," the man retorted with a crooked grin. "My business is making money, which means that since you're here, you'll buy something or get out."

Daxton grunted and looked around while Brent kept checking his hair for spiders.

The old man grunted in return, losing his patience.

"Time's up. Shop's closed. Get out," the shopkeeper demanded, pushing the boys out of the caravan and slamming the door.

"How rude," Daxton fumed.

"I agree," Brent concurred, jumping at everything that crawled by.

A hooded figure dressed in a long black coat walked their way. They ducked down beside the wagon, waiting to see who it might be.

The hooded figure knocked three times. The shopkeeper opened the blinds and then let the hooded figure in. Daxton moved to one of the tiny, broken windows. Looking in, he saw Morpheus.

"Morpheus is in there," Daxton whispered as he strained to hear the conversation going on inside.

"Master Morpheus. I didn't expect you this month," the shopkeeper chimed in a cheery tone. "What brings you to the shop today?"

"I need more of that dark licorice root like you supplied me last month," he requested. "The brewtion I made is not working and I need to make it stronger."

"Yes, of course. Did you brew it correctly?" he asked, pulling down a wooden box.

"Of course I did," Morpheus responded indignantly." I need you to double what you gave me last time.

"Oh? Big plans?"

"Yes."

Daxton saw Brent's eyes widen and he could tell that the wheels in his companion's head were turning. They watched as the shopkeeper put the longest root on the table and began to cut it up.

Brent pulled on Daxton's arm. "We have to go," he insisted.

"What do you think he was doing with that root?" Daxton asked when they were away from the shop. "I've never seen a black root like that. Where'd it come from?"

"Somewhere dark and mutated," Brent stated.

The two walked quickly, eager to get back to the cheerier section of the caravan.

Daxton took a breath, knowing it was getting late and Brent was right.

Somewhere dark and mutated, but what could it be used for and why?

They moved down the lane and turned left, then right, and then left again. Soon they approached a large colorful caravan, painted with red and white stripes. Popcorn was popping from the roof, and even the stairs were made from large kernels waiting to be popped. Painted in many different colors was the sign 'ELLA'S ELEMENTAL KERNELS.'

Inside were small chairs and out front was a table in the shape of kernels. Popcorn hung everywhere around the open tent. There were many different kinds of popcorn kernels in a glass display case; caramel apple, licorice, chicken, cheese, scream machine, and sassafras were some of the names that were written on the display case. A large popper behind the case churned out even more.

The boys saw Tiffany at the counter and entered.

"I would like some of that Pink Kernel," Tiffany said to a lady behind the counter wearing a hat with the name 'Miss Ella.'

"Of course," Miss Ella said, opening the glass panel.

Just as she did, Blaze flew in, landing on the tub of pink kernels. His body flamed on causing the kernels to pop. Pink popcorn began to flow out of the display. He took a bit and moved over to the tub filled with green kernels, then blue, orange. Dancing on each until all the popcorn was overflowing.

Miss Ella was absolutely shocked and couldn't understand why the kernels were popping. She kept apologizing as she tried to stop it. "Here, take as much as you want."

They all grabbed large bags of popcorn. Tiffany's eyes widened as she held her bag.

"Ow! This is so hot!" she yelped.

"What are you talking about? I can't feel it through the bag," Daxton said.

"My hand feels like it's on fire!"

Daxton smiled, remembering he had not been bothered by heat since Blaze was hatched.

"Hurry up," Raizy demanded, sipping a rainbow freeze as she walked in.

"Raizy, where did you get that?" Tiffany asked.

"Over at Six Elixirs. Iris and the others are still there."

"Okay, I'll be right back," Tiffany said, leaving.

"Tiffany, wait! Don't go by yourself!" Daxton yelled, but she was already gone.

Daxton got his sour popcorn and went outside to wait for the others. He arched his eyebrows while taking a bite as Amon, Zeke, and Nicholas walked over.

"What in the world are you drinking?" Brent wondered aloud.

"This is a Foaming Volcano," Nicholas declared, holding a large foaming beaker filled with a red-orange liquid.

"Did you get it from Six Elixirs?" asked Daxton.

"Yep," Amon responded, picking off a hardened piece of sugar. "It's my favorite shop."

"It has liquid elements that pour from really cool taps," Zeke remarked, taking a large gulp of his Foaming Volcano.

Daxton felt a chill over his neck as bumps rose on his skin. The air became thick, the lamp post lights flickered, and a whirl of dust circled around him. He heard girls talking about weird and dark dreams, but he tuned them out.

A girl's voice pleaded in Daxton's mind, *Help me.*

A scream was heard in the distance and without a word, he ran. The lamp post lights flickered out and the vendors left one by one, making loud popping noises as they vanished before his eyes. The pops continued to echo in his ears, even after the noise actually stopped. He shook his head, trying to focus on moving forward.

The girl's voice pleaded.

Hurry! He's coming!

Daxton was sure it was Tiffany. She was in terrible danger. He didn't know what was happening, but it couldn't be good. He had to get to her. He ran faster than he ever had before.

I'm coming, Tiffany! Daxton shouted in his mind, hoping she'd hear him too.

Lightning raged behind him as rain pelted him in the face. A moment ago, it wasn't raining, and now there was a terrible storm surrounding him. He didn't have time to think about it. He just had to get to her.

"Where are you?" Daxton yelled as the Six Elixirs wagon popped into thin air. Behind where the wagon was he saw a girl and ran toward her. Daxton needed to get to Tiffany and save her. As his hand reached the girl's shoulder, he tried to turn her around to fuss at her for leaving, but the girl didn't move. He moved around the frozen girl and saw a purple flower in her hair.

Iris.

Daxton's heart sank.

If this is Iris, where's Tiffany?

CHAPTER 24 - WHICH PATH TO TAKE

"Here! Iris is over here" Daxton yelled as he touched her cold hand.

The Beast! Where is Tiffany?

Daxton heard Madame Theresa arrive behind him. "Madame Theresa! Tiffany! The beast has her!"

"Daxton, calm down! The beast attacked Iris. Tiffany left must have left already. It would not have taken her with him. Now, please, I am dealing with a very serious situation," Madame Theresa said, looking at the children who had gathered around. Her eyes darted from child to child, then moved to the storm around them. It looked like she couldn't focus. "Quickly now, children, activate your bubbles and follow Preston back to Eldragor. The Rift, I'm afraid it might be back. Go! Now!"

Daxton watched many large bubbles appear, then disappear as the children jumped in them. He didn't want to leave. He knew something horrible had happened to Tiffany. There was no way she already went home. She couldn't make a bubble by herself. He knew he couldn't stay, though. It was getting worse by the second. Cracks in the ground were becoming gorges, quickly filled by the rain. His worst fears were coming true. Madame Theresa was right. The Rift was back.

"Home," he said, jumping into his bubble.

Daxton's muscles tightened up as he braced for the sensation. Closing his eyes, he was jerked forward as waves of nausea flew through him. Within a few moments, he landed in the great chamber. Brea and Blaze flew out of his satchel and soared above him, like guards.

Children were running around, panicked at what they had just seen.

"Raizy! Have you seen Tiffany?"

"No, and she isn't in our room."

Daxton couldn't handle this, not tonight. The emotions were becoming too much. He was scared. He was angry.

Where is she?

"Daxton, did you find Tiffany?" Brent asked, the panic clear on his face.

"No, but I will. You get everyone to our chamber. You all should be safe until Theresa returns."

"Where are you going?"

"To find Tiffany. Go!"

The Rift is here and I can't do anything. How can I if I can't even find my friend?

Brent nodded, ushering the other students through the barrier.

Daxton turned his attention to his air eleagon. "Brea! Find Tiffany!"

Brea shook her head, flying through the air barrier.

"Blaze, come!"

Blaze soared through the air, landing on Daxton's shoulder.

Brea was in investigation mode, flying up and down in a wave pattern, trying to catch Tiffany's scent. With each second, Daxton grew more and more scared. Brea was usually good at finding people or things, but she just kept moving, almost without any direction. She flew ahead of Daxton just enough to lead the way, her white wings expanding as she disappeared into the painting of the staircase on the large wall next to the actual staircase. It had always seemed out of place before, but Daxton couldn't believe what he had just seen. He squinted and ran forward. Brea was gone.

"Where'd she go?" he asked, his voice panicked.

Blaze took a deep breath and let out a little fireball, shooting it towards the lamp in the painting. The lamp lit up.

Daxton grabbed the golden frame and pulled himself up into it. The picture gave way and he was on a staircase leading down somewhere he'd never seen. He followed the torches down the stairs with Brea leading. Daxton paused at the bottom of the stairs, letting his eyes adjust.

Brea took off and followed the passageway straight to the end of the corridor and turned right into another passage.

"See anything, Brea?"

Brea shook her head no, flying ahead. She stopped at a ladder. He didn't even question it. He had to keep going.

Daxton climbed up the ladder and cautiously pushed on the door above his head. As he peeped under the door, he was outside the North Tower.

Looking out, he saw the hooded figure in the distance moving away from the grounds of Eldragor over the meadow toward the edge of the Pitch Forest.

Daxton hurried to catch up. At the edge of the forest, the hooded figure was greeted by a Vorous Beast, with what looked like a large bundle. Brea and Blaze growled

"Shh." He couldn't risk being seen yet.

The figure and beast disappeared deeper into the woods.

Daxton hurried after and was greeted with near darkness. Twigs brushed against his skin, but he barely even felt it. Something was happening here and he was going to find out what. Daxton focused on the noises made by the figure and was able to stay close.

Brea hovered close by, while Blaze flew ahead. His fiery mane lit the way. As they entered a clearing, they were confronted by a six-foot-tall black tornado.

Daxton's mind was in a muddle, confused at the deadly tornado coming straight for him. Hoping it would work, he arched his array high over his head and then brought his arms down quickly. His array spun to a blur and a force of air flew through the tornado and it was no more.

Surprised at his own power, Daxton was suddenly out of breath.

Obviously I used too much power on that, he thought before moving forward again, into even thicker woods.

No longer able to hear his quarry, Daxton had to rely on the eleagons to lead the way. Suddenly they came into a large clearing, and that's when he saw it: The Eternal Tree.

Dark red roots burst through the ground around it. On one side of the tree, a gooey glob of green algae covered the tree trunk. Hot blue bubbles popped on the surface of the opposite side, releasing a foul stench. Its black leaves were heavy with tar that slowly dripped to the ground below. Its trunk seemed to reach into the darkness above.

Its dying was all Daxton could think as he moved closer with his eleagons.

They could feel the darkness pressing down on them. Even as the eleagons paused, Daxton was drawn closer. Shadows danced all around Daxton as he moved ahead very quietly and very slowly. The warmth of his pendant felt comforting on his chest as he approached the tree. There he saw the vorous beast with the figure standing beside it, lit by a torch's light.

That isn't Morpheus.

CHAPTER 25 - ALL WILL BE REVEALED

"Sengal?" Daxton asked, his eyes adjusting to the darkness.

"Welcome, Daxton," Sengal said in a raspy voice.

Daxton stood still as the Eternal Tree's black roots began to crawl around the ground like snakes. He noticed a pale body lying in the mud near the tree. The person wasn't moving at all, and soon, the roots leaped up like an octopus, attaching themselves to the person's motionless limbs. He couldn't tell who it was until he saw the blonde hair.

Tiffany!

Daxton's heart raced as his mind registered what was happening. The life was being drained from her right before his eyes. He had to save her. Scanning the area, he saw Sengal just standing there by the tree, waiting on something. "What do you want?" Daxton asked, taking a quick step toward Tiffany.

Sengal's dark green eyes glanced at Daxton as a sincere smile cracked. "Power!" he replied, taking his hand to the tree trunk. "Justice." He shifted to the right as a bubble popped. "And the Master of Darkness to finish The Rift." He moved forward, placing his other hand on the tree.

"The Rift! It will destroy us all!" Daxton said, inching closer.

"Only the weaker ones," Sengal said, snapping his fingers and summoning a vine to grab Daxton's feet and arms.

"You're, uh, you're helping him start the Rift! You're helping Vulkan?" Daxton asked, fighting the vines.

Sengal laughed. "No, no."

"Then who?"

"Stupid boy! You will see!" Sengal responded gleefully, rubbing his dirty hands together and then moving to a large root unearthed from the ground. "For His Darkness," he said, snapping his fingers. A thorny vine rose up and slashed Sengal's palm and blood dripped onto the Eternal Tree's roots. The roots simmered as the blood coated the dark bark, traveling like water and feeding the roots that connected to Tiffany's limbs.

The ground shook and the tree began to breathe; in and out in repetition. Sengal collapsed next to it. Daxton couldn't believe what he was seeing. And then, two eyes within the tree opened.

A tree-like hand formed, then legs emerged from the trunk. The awkward body shifted, pulling away from the tree, like a shoe with gum pulling away from the pavement, until a bony body appeared, draped in a thin black veil. The man had black hair, a short nose, and a long face resembling a horse. Shadows moved around him. Through the shadows, a black staff with a glowing red skull appeared. Black roots from the tree were still attached to his ankles and a limb was still attached to his elbow.

Daxton trembled as the man moved toward him. He had seen him before in his dreams.

"Well, that's not the welcome I expected," the man's eerie voice said as his hands curved over his face, feeling it. His open eyes revealed nothing but darkness.

"Who are you?" Daxton asked, though he feared he knew the answer.

"I am Lord Dominus," he said, walking forward, breaking a limb that held his arm to the tree.

"Lord Dominus," Daxton stuttered. "Annya defeated you! How are you even here?"

"How was it that she was able to defeat me is the better question."

"She was more powerful than you!"

"Was she? Or was it someone else? Someone who was not to return but did? Oh! Yes! How indeed am I here? It's been twelve years since I have been able to draw breath in my human elemental form. If it hadn't been for my vorous beasts, I would have been stuck in the tree forever. They found the one thing that would start my transformation. The one thing that was stolen from me," Lord Dominus paused, eyeing Daxton. "My array!"

Daxton froze.

His array? How could someone do that?

"Who took it?" Daxton asked, amazed that he even had a voice right now.

"Annya Luxador, or so I thought! When she banished me into this tree, she had no idea the events that would occur. As the tree grew weaker, I grew stronger. Vulkan and his methods were making me stronger. I knew the Eternal Tree was on the brink of destruction, and he would keep feeding it. Feeding me power. As soon as that girl here takes her final breath, I will be able to finally take back what's mine. Oh look, you have eleagons."

"Tiffany has nothing to do with this," Daxton said, glaring at Lord Dominus.

"You don't know, do you?" Lord Dominus said in an eerie tone. "Oh, she has everything to do with this. She has MY ARRAY!"

Time was running out and Daxton knew it. With every declaration, Lord Dominus was getting angrier. Daxton weighed his options, took a deep breath, and turned his hidden wrist over, illuminating his array. It beamed brightly in the darkness. Slowly, he twirled his fingers behind his back letting the wind build for a sneak attack. With a fast swing of his arm and flick of his wrist, Daxton released a tornado at Lord Dominus and started running over to where Tiffany was, jumping over cracks and dodging tree branches, all the while adding to the strength of the tornado.

"Going to have to do better than that, Daxton Tanner!" Lord Dominus yelled as he illuminated his array and built an angled wall of earth that diverted the tornado around himself and into the distance, beyond the reach of Daxton's power. "You won't be able to save her. I am getting stronger. She's getting weaker!"

Daxton cupped his hands together, moved them back and forth, and shot air blasts at the roots in front of him to make a path toward Tiffany. The roots holding Tiffany rose up and lifted her in the air. Daxton had to think, and he had to act fast.

"Brea, I need steps!"

Brea nodded and puffed. With each breath, a cloud formed. The steps were small, but Daxton didn't have a choice.

"That's my girl," Daxton said, jumping on the first one then the next. He was about to move to the third when a root grabbed his ankle. It was like a hand burning through his skin.

"Blaze! The roots!"

Blaze flapped his wings, blowing a fireball straight at the root, which shriveled back, not breaking completely, but it didn't move forward again. The smell of burnt wood wafted through the air.

Ignoring the smell and the pain in his ankle, Daxton kept moving forward. With one more cloud to go, he finally reached Tiffany. It was like the roots were embedded in her skin. They were in her arms, legs, and palms. He pulled the roots from her limbs. Small trickles of bright red blood emerged from where the limbs once were.

"NO!" Lord Dominus yelled, his voice echoing throughout the chamber.

"Brea, bed!"

Brea darted around the air, creating a cool breeze until clouds formed. They were larger and thicker than the steps. These bright clouds would easily hold his friend. Daxton picked Tiffany up and laid her on top of the bed.

"Daxton, you found me," she whispered, barely opening her

eyes. Her voice was scratchy, in desperate need of water, but she was safe.

"Always," Daxton responded, and looked to Brea. "Get her out of here!"

Brea tried to blow her and the clouds to safety, but a root was still attached to her ankle.

"Just one more," Daxton said.

"Get the eleagons!" Lord Dominus's voice boomed, echoing through Daxton's skull.

A large vorous beast launched towards Brea, who growled before moving. She was faster than the beast. It barely had time to react as she dug her paws in one of the beast's eyes, blinding it. A smile curved to her face as her tail went to the beast's head, smacking it.

"Go! Get to safety!" Daxton yelled, trying to pull the root free from Tiffany.

The eleagons flew high, dodging left then right. While he watched the eleagons, roots wrapped around his own body, grabbing his legs and arms. He was pulled back down by the snake-like roots, and his eyes hazed over as a large root with thorns pierced the back of his hand. Daxton screamed in pain as the vine split his skin. Blood poured out of his hand and onto the roots holding him down. He could not control his array illuminating from his palm.

Violent winds roared around him, ready to attack their prey. The wicked roots pierced Daxton's skin, their mighty thorns seeping into his veins. As the roots entered his body, his hands started to turn black, his eyes dulled over, and his skin rippled with blackness. Even his blonde hair was now a shade of death.

Daxton had no idea what to expect and just wanted it to be over, but then pain tore through him again as the roots began ripping a section of his array apart. With each violent tug, he yelled in pain as the elemental life was ripped from him. He watched his beautiful array spin away from him like sharp pieces of broken stained glass.

Pain coursed through the young elementor. Brea flew back into the madness. She planted her paws into the root as her white form started to turn black. With a desperate breath, she shot an air blast at the root to try and free Daxton. As she destroyed the root, three more bound her next to the young elementor.

Blaze shot fireballs at the roots, but like Brea, he was overwhelmed by the sheer amount. His body lit up in a giant flame. Brea blew into the fire, expanding it even more, burning many roots, but others circled them and smacked them to the ground. They weren't moving.

I am going to die without knowing if my mother ever loved me or if she just tossed me away during that storm. If my mother left me to die, then what difference does it matter now? I am on borrowed time.

He gazed up at the Eternal Tree, no longer frightened. Somewhere deep down he knew he was going to die, and this was just how it was going to be. Even if his heart didn't stop beating, he knew that a part of him was going to die and never be the same again.

Daxton felt as if he was drowning, unable to breathe, unable to see. All he could do was feel pain, lots of unending pain. With each violent rip, Daxton jerked in pain. He could take it. He had to take it. The longer Lord Dominus focused on him, the longer Tiffany had to survive.

Dominus began to laugh as he took a step toward Daxton. "This will be over for you soon. Once I get the girl's array, you won't have to worry about anything at all. Just rest now. You've been a great help."

Another dark vine slowly made its way to the base of Daxton's neck. He waited for what he knew was going to come. In an instant, he felt the vine pierce the nape of neck, sucking the elemental life from him.

As all of the elemental energy was pulled from Daxton, the Eternal Tree shifted back to a more forgiving form. Buds began to bloom on the branches of the strengthening tree.

"Please, please make the pain stop," Daxton cried, as blood dripped from his palm. His tears hit his pendant, causing it to glow.

In that desperate plea, help was granted.

"Oh, Daxton, I told you to stay away," a tiny voice scolded as small purple wings flapped back and forth and a spixie landed near his head. As her wings fluttered, the wind gathered around Lord Dominus. The spixie then blew purple dust at Lord Dominus, who yelled out as he was momentarily blinded.

Daxton looked at his palm, still turning black.

What did I do?

"Stay safe, child," the spixie spoke before flying away.

Theresa, Morpheus, and Vulkan arrived suddenly and took in the madness. They looked at each other, knowing what each needed to do, and moved out from one another.

"AURATORATION!" Madame Theresa yelled as her array spun. The air moved around her so fast, a tornado formed from the very air she breathed. The tip of the violent cyclone ripped and roared, gaining speed. The destruction was headed for its one target: Lord Dominus.

"Theresa! Still angry?" Lord Dominus said in a mocking tone as he held out his hands and summoned the vorous beast to his aid. With each hand out, he absorbed one on the left and one on the right. His fingers twirled and out spun a small black array, creating a violent shadow tornado, mirroring the one in front of him. "Just a bit more!" he yelled, yielding the shadow tornado towards Theresa's tornado. A crack was heard as Lord Dominus was almost fully freed from the Eternal Tree.

Daxton screamed as the roots of the tree continued to pierce his limbs, attaching to him. With each attack, his face strained more and more.

I can't do this anymore.

"Theresa, you can't hold him!" Morpheus yelled, illuminating his black array.

"I have to! All chaos will break loose if he is freed!" Madame Theresa yelled, summoning the tornado to yield to the left.

"Cover me!" Morpheus yelled as he snapped his fingers, calling his shadow to aid him. "Vulkan, get the Negment!"

Morpheus's shadow crouched low, moving behind Dominus, distracting him.

Theresa was doing a dance with her hands, summoning more air to fight the shadow tornado, but it matched her power.

"Wasteful boy! What did you do?" Morpheus said, pulling black roots out of Daxton's limbs.

Daxton whelped in pain as white foam bubbled from his mouth, the sounds from the battle echoing in his ears.

"Theresa, don't harm the tree!" Vulkan yelled, slinging his array forward to burn the thorny roots that entangled Tiffany.

"I will see you all soon enough," Lord Dominus's voice echoed as he broke the last root from his ankle, getting free.

The roots around him lost life as Lord Dominus erupted into shadows.

Brea and Blaze shook off their roots and flew over to Morpheus, who was carrying Daxton. His eyes glazed over as Brea laid on his chest, nestling the pendant. Blaze rested his head on Daxton's black palm, trying to heal it.

Madame Theresa stood between the two men with the children in their arms, the roots on the ground crawling away again like snakes. The wind was howling, and Daxton felt a coldness slither down his spine as a wisp of wind echoed through his ear.

"You can't save them. You can't save anyone," an eerie voice echoed in Daxton's head.

"Hall of Healing!" Madame Theresa said, grabbing Daxton's right wrist and Tiffany's left. Her array formed all around the five.

Daxton saw a blur before he heard a loud crack.

Safe. Tiffany is safe.

CHAPTER 26 - IS IT TRUE?

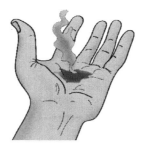

Daxton rolled over in his bed. To his right was a calendar. It showed today was Thursday.

Exams!

He had missed them. He pulled the sheets back and there he saw it dead in the center of his palm: a black ring. His palms hurt, the pain struck him deep in his core. He felt empty, like he had given away something great that he would never get back. Looking at the dark spot in the center of his palm, Daxton had hoped just maybe his array would appear. Taking a deep breath, he closed his eyes, concentrating hard. As he did, the black ring burned and he closed his palm. It was like a thousand shards of glass ran through his body. While he hated the pain, it was a reminder of what he had done and what he survived. It would serve as a reminder of Eldragor.

"Ah, Daxton, you're awake," Ambassador Vulkan said, entering suddenly. Brea and Blaze, who were resting on Daxton's bed, raised their heads at the visitor.

"Yes, Ambassador," Daxton said, closing his palm tight. Realizing Brea and Blaze were visible, he tried to hide them from Vulkan, still unsure of what he would do to them.

"Don't worry about them," Vulkan said, raising his hand slightly. Brea moved toward him, and Vulkan began to pet her. "No harm will come to them. I know eleagons have a bad reputation for what they have done in the past, but these two have proven themselves."

"Proven?" Daxton asked.

"Yes, you see, because they saved you, they are inherently good. These are two eleagons we never should have to worry about. I've sensed that since you've been here. I never felt danger from them, so there was never a need to interfere."

Daxton breathed a sigh of relief.

But what had Lord Dominus meant? Those eleagons?

"Now for the reason I'm really here. Sengal has been helping Lord Dominus for years," Ambassador Vulkan stated. "Sengal was not fully to blame. We all ignored my brother, which made it easier for Dominus to use Sengal's desires and dreams against him and take control. I will not let that happen again."

"That is good news, I guess," Daxton said. "How was this all possible?"

"When Annya trapped him in the tree all those years ago, she couldn't trap all of his evil. Beasts roamed the grounds, feeding on children and their arrays. We thought we had destroyed them all, or at least forced them out of the training academy, but Sengal befriended one of the beasts. He knew their power and why they were here. He decided he would use them to help find Lord Dominus's array in the Normal Lands."

"Is that why the beast was there in the woods before Madame Theresa found us?"

"Yes, the vorous beast sensed children with arrays. If she had not gotten there in time, the beast would have been able to feast."

"How do you know all of this?" Daxton asked.

"Sengal confessed to everything. The darkness took hold and he couldn't stop it. I can't believe I had been aiding this for years."

Daxton didn't know what to say.

Were there others here he couldn't trust because of Lord Dominus's power?

"I wanted to thank you for what you did. You gave the Eternal Tree your array. It was powerful enough to stabilize the tree. You risked your life and saved us."

Daxton nodded. "What about Lord Dominus?"

"Lord Dominus will always be a threat. For now, the Veil of Darkness is gone, thanks to you."

A knock sounded on the door.

"You have visitors," Vulkan said with a small smile as he left.

Daxton's friends barged through the white door, each helping to carry a huge get-well basket filled with fluffy cotton candy, cheese, and rolls cut in the shape of clouds, as well as other assorted goodies.

What does one say when they have survived death.

"Hello?"

Blaze flew over to get some floating cotton candy. Looking around, Daxton saw Tiffany's bright smile.

I am glad see is alright. How did Annya give her Lord Dominus's array?

"Yay, you're awake!" Tiffany said excitedly. "Thank you, Daxton, you saved me!" She hugged him tightly. "I am all cured and look at this!"

She lifted her hand and turned her palm. A light red circle illuminated from the center.

"That's amazing, Tiffany. What is all this?" Daxton asked, rubbing his temples as he looked at the basket.

"We have all come to wish you good luck and say thank you," Raizy said, smiling.

"Thanks," Daxton said.

"Tiffany told us what you did. It is just really awesome of you, man," Amon said.

"Thanks," Daxton said again.

"This is an extra gear that Mr. Hopkins says will bring good luck," Nicholas said, handing Daxton a copper gear.

"Thanks," Daxton said, turning it in his hand. What else was he supposed to say?

"I, er, I mean we missed you," Halo said, smiling. "I'm glad you are doing better."

"We all passed," Bjorn said. "I did better than Halo, by the way, but we all will be back."

"Congratulations," Daxton said, sadly realizing that if he had no array he couldn't come back. This was it for him in Eldragor.

"Oh, Daxton," said Raizy, realizing the same thing as Daxton. "Giving up your array the way you did was really brave."

"Thanks, Raizy," Daxton said, beaming a fake smile. In truth, he wanted to cry.

"I will never forget you," Raizy said, giving him a hug.

"All right, everyone, that's enough," Madame Theresa ordered, walking in. "I need a few words alone with Daxton. You have less than an hour to enjoy the rest of the festival."

"Bye, Daxton," they said in a sad tone as they left one by one, giving him a final hug.

"Tiffany, Brent, you two go say your goodbyes before we take off to the Normal Lands."

"Yes, ma'am," they said, following the rest out.

"What you did was very brave, Daxton, but I must tell you that it came at a great price. Your air array is gone."

Daxton ran his fingers over his palm, nodding.

"I am afraid that without an array, you will not be able to return to Eldragor to finish your training," she stated in a sad tone, taking her hand to Daxton's face.

251

Daxton felt weak, sad, and alone. Again. Always alone. His hand found the comfort of Brea and Blaze. "I understand," he said behind a masked smile.

"The eleagons will remain yours," she said.

"But I thought they needed to be near their natural element. They'll only get that here." He began to panic. He lost so much. He couldn't lose them too.

"While usually true, something has changed about these two. Perhaps they were exposed to something in the tree or to the destruction of your array, but they will be strong enough to travel home with you. Also, don't forget that they were hatched there, not here. I am not certain you will remember these events because the loss of an array affects people differently."

"I understand," Daxton said.

"Know that you are a hero and we will always be indebted to you. I am so sorry, Daxton."

Blaze moved to Daxton's palm, resting his head against it. Daxton felt the warmth.

"All might not be lost," Theresa said with a slight smile. "We never did get to learn what the quill saw. I must go get ready for our trip," she said, leaving the room quickly.

Daxton rubbed his palm with a smile of hope.

Soon he was on his way home.

As the top of the orphanage came into view from the bket, Daxton's mind raced. The pendant on his chest warmed him as a silent tear rolled down his cheek and fell on it. His adventure had come to an end.

Was it worth it? Maybe the tree is permanently stabilized.

Seeing the smile on Tiffany's face, he knew it was the right decision. Holding his satchel tight and feeling the weight of the pendant, he knew he would never forget.

The bket landed. Tiffany and Brent grabbed their luggage and jumped out, excited to be home.

Daxton frowned. Madame Theresa put her hand on Daxton' shoulder.

He turned around and gave her a hug, "Thank you," he whispered and exited the bket.

"No, thank you," Madame Theresa said. With a flick of her wrist, she and the bket took off and were soon hidden by clouds.

Daxton hurried and caught up with Tiffany and Brent, and the friends soon passed the old oak. Daxton smiled, seeing Mrs. Pat watering her white roses.

"Snakes! The snakes are back!" Mrs. Pat screamed.

The trio smiled at one another.

CRACK!

Daxton's hands went to his pendant, cradling it.

Tiffany looked at Daxton, "Oh no, two is enough!"

The End.

Made in the USA
Columbia, SC
02 December 2021